STONE BABY

And more strange tales

by

Nikki Nelson-Hicks

Front cover image by Brenna Gael

First printing edition 2021

ISBN 978-1-7349343-1-1

Third Crow Press
640 Bradford Drive
Gallatin, TN 37066

nikkinelsonhicks@gmail.com

A quick note…

Hello, there!

In your hands is a collection of short, dark, and nasty stories. It has been my honored privilege to be your narrator (albeit metaphysically) and it is my deepest wish that you enjoy my humble offerings.

I hope you are warm, safe, sane, and well. I imagine you curled up in a favorite chair or in lying comfortably your bed. Taking some time to read a story or two before giving yourself over to the blessed arms of Morpheus.

Oh, dear.

Are you sure you want to be reading *these* stories?

Oh, well. Caveat emptor.

NNH, 2021

COON HUNT

3

For Brian

"See this scar?" Grandpa asked as he pushed up his sleeve. "I got that during a coon hunt back in '32." The porch creaked as he leaned back in his ladderback rocking chair. His young grandson sat nestled in his lap, waiting for a story, while the rest of the family prepared Sunday dinner inside the house. "Biggest damn one we ever treed. And mean! Lord, I'll remember that one for the rest of my days. The way it fought and scratched and cursed. OOOWEEE! It was a sight!"

"My daddy went hunting once and brought back a deer head." the little boy piped in. "Mom got all mad."

Grandpa shook his head laughing and looked down at the boy, "Let me tell you something, boy," he leaned forward, his head cocked. "Your Paw don't know nothin' about coon huntin'." He sat back and snorted. "Hmmph! He calls hisself a hunter. Boy, there's more to huntin' than running out into the woods with a six pack of beer in one hand and a rifle in the other. Nah......these young ones today..... don't know nothing of huntin'..of the chase."

"But...my Paw...he knew. And he taught me....listen up-

"There was always a mess of them running across my Paw's back field so we would set up traps, wooden stakes- oh, about as big around as your leg and half as long, boy- all around the back side, pointy side up. Paw and my Uncle Jed had trained the dogs to corral the coons especially through this strip of land. It was one of my Paw's favorite tricks."

"My dog can do tricks. Roll over, fetch, shake…all kinds of stuff. Ginger is a good dog."

"You wouldn't want nothing to do with these dogs, boy! These dogs weren't for petting. These dogs were for huntin'! They were the meanest pack of hounds I ever knew.

You could hear those dogs baying all over the hills as soon as they caught wind of those coons. Then….Good Lord! You couldn't hold them back! They'd bolt right after them and run 'em straight to the stakes. You could hear the coons a'screamin' as soon as they'd hit'em. Usually, we'd trap the bastards right there in the stakes but that one in '32 was a mean one. It just kept running, blood trailing everywhere it went. But that was just fine by us 'cause the dogs would get a whiff and chase it all the harder. Lordy, that one in '32 was a smart one and kept just ahead of the pack. I figure we must've trailed that devil almost half the night."

"I remember camping outside in the back yard all night with my friends. It's so dark out here in the country at night. How did you all see to hunt?"

"The moon was full that night, I recall. Shining like a yellow beacon. Besides, hounds don't depend on their eyes for huntin'. They use their sniffers." he said, tapping the side of his thin nose. "It's better than radar."

The boy laughed. "Cool."

"He'd run plumb through Paw's entire 10 acre field and smack into the old county graveyard. Stupid thing had tripped over a gravestone and damn near broke a leg. Since it was my first trip out- I was all of 12 at the time – my Uncle Jed figured he'd let me do the honors. Somethin' of an old tradition….my first blood."

"Kinda like how last year, when I first turned six, my daddy let me hook my first worm at the Shelby Park fishing rodeo?"

"Hmmmm. Something like that."

The boy nodded, understanding.

"So I stepped forward, my rope in my hand, proud as a peacock, when…suddenly, all hell broke loose! The damn fool started hollarin' and clawin' at the ground, throwin' sticks and a stones, anything that could be found on the ground. I raised up my arm just in time to avoid catching a rock right in the eye. That's where I got this scar from."

Grandpa stopped and pointed down again to the scar. The skin around it puckered like stitches in a hastily sewn hem. The boy leaned closer to study it, touching it gingerly. "Ewwww!"

Grandpa sat back. "Well, we put up with enough that old coon. We picked up some good sized sticks and went in to beat some sense into the creature's head. But it kept on throwin' and screamin' at us like were were a pack of wild dogs. I was fixing to go in after it but my Uncle Jed pulled me aside and got out his shotgun. After that, it was easy to drag it over to an old oak tree and hang it up proper."

"Wow. Did you get to keep it?" the boy asked.

The old man sighed and tussled his grandson's hair. "Boy, you don't know nothin' about coon huntin'."

The End

A VERY

GOOD YEAR

For The Birthday Girl, J.P.

Her head swam with colors and memories. She was a fetus, her knees up to her chin, wrapped in strong linen and encased inside an oak ribbed womb. It tightened as steam swirled up between the oak planks, bringing with it smells of plum, raspberry, and chocolate. She blinked as-

It was noon on Jackie's birthday, and she stood outside a marble building, biting her lip and flicking the gilded corner of an invitation.

She had received the invitation in her mailbox a week ago. There was no postmark or return address. Inside the envelope was the gold lined card that invited the bearer to a glorious birthday, all expenses paid, at the exclusive day spa and winery, Joie De Vivre. There was a handwritten note that said, "A woman grows more delicious the longer she ripens on the vine."

Jackie looked at her reflection in the mirrored storefront and smirked at the sentiment. She sucked in her cheeks and pulled at the loose skin on her neckline and shook her head. It was her fiftieth birthday. She had spent a half century on this hunk of rock spiraling around the sun. That is eighteen thousand, two hundred and fifty days of wear and tear on a vehicle made entirely of bone, meat and water. And that wasn't counting leap years. "Maybe a day at the spa is exactly what I need."

There wasn't a door handle on the clear mirrored wall just two slots with brass plaques. The one on the right read WHITE CARD and one on the left read GOLD CARD.

Jackie shrugged and slid her card into the GOLD CARD slot.

The sweat rolled into her eyes. The plink plink plink sounds of dripping echoed off the chamber walls. The heat and pressure increased. Unable to scream, her mouth sewn shut and full of sweet merlot grapes, she choked on-

A door opened and a bright smiling woman in a white lab coat and clipboard greeted her warmly. "Welcome! Welcome! Please come in!" She wrapped one arm around Jackie's shoulders and escorted her into a gleaming, empty, white hallway towards a reception desk. "My name is Rachel and I'll be your guide today. You look absolutely radiant." She put her nose deeply into Jackie's hair and sniffed. "Is that your natural hair color?"

"Uh, no…"

Rachel frowned and made a check on her clipboard. "No worries. Let me get your sampling kit and we'll get started."

She went behind the desk and pulled out a white plush bathrobe, slippers and a white satin bag. She handed them all to Jackie. "Raoul will take you to the back where they will take blood, stool and urine samples. The specimen bottles are in the bag. Okay? Okay. Then you can go to your special spa room where you will strip off your clothes, take a sterilizing hydrobath, and then put on the robe and slippers. Once that is all done, you can relax with a complimentary plate of cheese, chocolate to nibble on and plenty of wine waiting for you. Okay? Okay. Ah, here he is!"

"Hello." A beautiful dark man with flowing black hair came over and took Jackie by the hand. He lifted her arm and looked at her with an appraising eye. "She looks robust with underlying earthy tones, yes?"

"Definitely. The hair isn't natural but the underlying melodies definitely dance on the top."

"Well, let's not count the tannins before they pop, yes? Come with me, please."

"Wait." Jackie took her hand away. "What do you need with my blood and stool?"

Rachel blinked both eyes together, tilted her head and smiled, widely. "To adjust your spa treatment to your own special genetic markers, silly. Raoul will take good care of you. He's one of our finest masseuse and sommeliers. Go on now. I have to go. I see there is another guest at the Gold Card door. It's going to be a bumper crop!"

Raoul took her to a small but cozy room. There was a small couch and a table with food. On the wall were prints of a French vineyards framed to look like faux windowsills.

"Please, undress and put on the robe and slippers. The nurses will be with you very soon."

-the memories. The beaky nosed nurse who took her blood and grimaced at the color of her urine. The nurse with the bobble head who nodded at every question and held her hand when someone bent her over a table and swiped her rectum with a twelve inch cotton swap. And then there were the shots...so many needles....

"How are you feeling?" Raoul said. "Are you starting to feel relaxed?"

"Relaxed? What the hell was that? All that poking and probing. It was humiliating!"

"Hmmm. Usually our guests are more relaxed by this time."

"The shower nearly took my skin off! If I were paying for this, I'd sue!"

Raoul nodded. "Aw, yes. Tenacious. You are an earthy blend, aren't you? Don't worry. It's all part of the preparation. The results will be ready soon and then we'll know the correction portions and suitable alkaline settings for the mixture." Raoul smiled and took Jackie back to his small but cozy room. "Please, stay here until I come for you. Settle in and relax. There is plenty of water to drink and fresh fruit, cheese and chocolate for you to dine on."

"Water? What about the wine? Rachel said there would be plenty of wine."

"Oh, no. Not until we get the results of your pH balance. Until then, please, drink only the filtered water we have provided for you."

"Well, this is bullshit! What does my pH have to do with getting a massage? Why did I have to give blood for a facial? And I don't even want to know why you needed to poke around in my asshole. No, I don't care if this takes years off my face and gives me the tits of a twenty-year-old, I've had it." Jackie started taking off her bathrobe. "I'm out of here. Just give me back my clothes. Wait…. whoa…what the hell…" The room shifted and Jackie fell on her ass.

"That took long enough." Raoul checked his watch and made a notation on his clipboard.

There was a snap and then another. A rib? An arm? Her body was squeezed and twisted like a sponge and yet she remained alive and conscious enough to hear the plink, plink, plink of her essence drip into the vat below. She raged against her stupid stubbornness to live…what had he called her? Tenacious.

There was no pain. No, that would taint the aftertaste. She remembered hearing someone say that. "Her tannin level will be audacious enough to break the Spring Valley Spa record!"

They had laughed at that.

Before they'd even finished the job of murdering her, they had laughed.

Audacious? Jackie let a grin slid across her lips, splitting the threads that kept her mouth sewn shut. Fuck that.

She'd give then TENACIOUS.

She took a deep breath through her nose and pressed down, using all the muscles she'd learned to use during childbirth. She pushed and pushed until she felt the hatred flow through her,

Plink, Plink.

PLUNK.

Out and into the vat below.

The End

15

THE TIPPING POINT

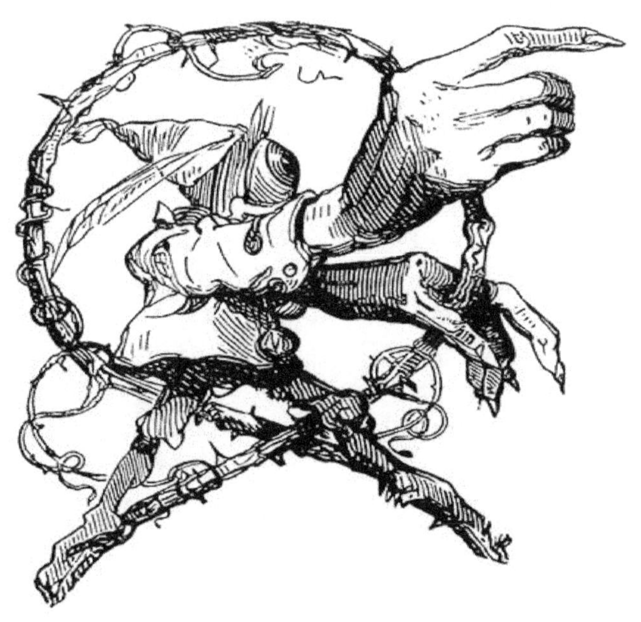

For my awkward geeky friends

TK, MY, AB, AR

"What did I tell you, son? Kids ain't nothing but a ticket to poverty. Shit. I figured it was the best thing about being a faggot."

Goddammit, Mom. Shane imagined her, sitting in the kitchen, wearing a second-hand silk bathrobe she got from Goodwill, blowing smoke through a crack in the window, the rim of her coffee cup kissed with purple lipstick. He had no idea what color her hair was this week; she changed it more than she changed bedsheets. He took a deep breath and counted to ten like his therapist back in California told him.

"Mom, I need you to do this one thing for me. Please. I have an interview tomorrow."

"A job? Whose gonna hire a drunk with a record like you?"

"It's an opportunity. I need you to watch Kyle for a few hours, that's all."

"What if the kid has a fit or something?"

"The seizure medication is working fine now, thanks for asking."

"Ain't it got school or something?"

Shane let the word *it* roll off his back. "School is out for break."

"Well, shit. Why me? Fuck. Ask one of your queens."

Shane pushed the anger down, down deep. The memory of his friend, D'Angelo, laughing in his face saying, *"Nobody told you and Marcus to be breeders. Tough titty, little kitty."* was too fresh.

"Everyone else is busy. It's just a few hours. Look, I'll even throw in a bottle of Jack Daniels."

"Shit. Fine. I'll do it this once but, Shane, for Chrissakes, you need to have a rethink about being a daddy and let that shit go. Bring the kid over."

Breathe….breathe. "Mom, you have to pick him up. I don't have a car."

"So, get a ride. There's an app. Margo at the bar uses it all the time."

"If I could afford that, I'd hire a babysitter."

"Well, fuck! I have to do everything, just like always! Just when I thought I'd be free, you gone off to California, leaving me here to do as I please but, no! Here you come back into my life, like I owe you something. Let me tell you something, Little Miss Swish, I don't owe you noth-"

Shane ending the call. He knew how it ended; he'd heard it for the first twenty years of his life.

"S'getti's ready to pour out, Daddy." Kyle said, wringing his hands. He was only seven and already knew how to cook more meals than Shane.

"Good. I'm hungry. At the table or in front of the tv?"

"Table. S'getti is messy."

Shane poured the pasta into the strainer and dished out the slippery noodles onto the plates. Kyle spooned out the sauce and sprinkled parmesan cheese on top of the red, meaty mound.

"I'll set the table. Spiderman or Superman glass?"

"Spiderman."

"Excellent choice. Now go wash your hands."

"Okay."

Shane watched Kyle walk to the bathroom. The 800 square foot, one bedroom apartment was a sharp drop from the four-bedroom, three-bathroom, full kitchen with a breakfast nook and hot tub on the deck bungalow they had in California. A lot of things had taken a dive since Marcus decided that being a husband and father wasn't what he wanted to do with his time. "Life's too short to be just *this*," he said before leaving. And then came the doubt, the chorus of his mother's voice that would only shut up after a few drinks that, before Shane knew it, turned into a few bottles. He bought our Marcus' share of their coding business and managed to tank the entire thing within 18 months. Embezzled from the employee's pension fund to keep up appearances and tanked the whole thing within 18 months. Only the grace of God kept him from doing time. The house went soon after. And here he was, back home and begging his cunt of a mother for a few hours attention, the circle complete.

Shane's hands trembled as he set down the plates. God, what he'd give for a drink.

Kyle slid into his seat with barely a word. He was a slender kid with a dancer's grace. Beautiful brown eyes, auburn hair and a snaggled tooth grin that melted Shane's heart every time. How could Marcus leave this?

"How's it going, kiddo?"

"Okay."

Kyle twirled the spaghetti around his fork. Shane noticed that the boy's nails were nibbled down to the wick. Kyle only did that when he was stressed. A sharp jab of worry pierced his gut. He thought he'd kept his son shielded from the mess they were in. As long as he didn't start pulling out his eyebrows again…Jesus, what a mess.

"Hey, guess what? I've got good news. I've got an interview tomorrow."

"Really? A job?"

"Yep, a real job that could be a big opportunity for me. For us, I mean. Except I'm going to need a favor from you. A big one."

"What?"

"Nobody is available to babysit so I need you to be the man of the house. Just for a few hours. Can you do that?"

Kyle stabbed at his spaghetti with his fork. "Why can't I go to your mom's house?"

He never called her Grandma. "She's not feeling too good right now. She's got a cold." Shane fell back onto old lies he used as a kid to explain why Mom couldn't come to PTA/teacher conferences/etc.

"Uh-huh." The boy looked up through thick lashes. There was no fooling this kid, thought Shane. "How long will you be gone?"

"Just for a few hours. You can sleep in. Or, how about this? What if I put the TV in your room? Just for the day."

"No, it's okay." Kyle's shoulders bunched up. " I'd rather watch TV in the living room."

"What's wrong?"

"I dunno. My old room was just better. This one smells weird."

"Yeah, I know. Things have been really different from California but if I get this job, I'll get us a new house just like our old house." That was a lie. This new job would barely help him to afford an extra bedroom. "And you'll have a TV and all sorts of stuff, just like back home. So, do we have a deal? You stay here by yourself while I go and get us a job?

Kyle shrugged.

"Come on, buddy, you know the rules. You've got my back and I've got yours." Shane put up his fist for a bump as he finished the chant. "Forever and ever, right?"

"You and me. Forever." The boy bumped his dad's fist. His slender fingers looked fragile.

"Ok, Dad, but can I ask for a favor?"

"Sure, ask away."

"Can I sleep with you on the futon tonight?"

Shane shook his head. "You're a big boy now." *A big boy that wets the bed. Stress induced incontinence said the therapist. Thanks, Doc, slide another knife in my back while you're there.* "Big boys sleep alone."

"Like you?"

Another stab. "Yeah. Just like me."

****

It was nearly midnight when Shane stealthily extracted himself from Kyle's bed. It was a bedtime routine that started after Marcus left. After a bedtime story and some chitchat about the day and plans for tomorrow, they would snuggle until Kyle fell asleep. Some nights, the boy would fall asleep quickly and sneaking out was a breeze. But tonight was a challenge. Kyle pleaded for "one more story…one more story!" The boy fought sleep like a tiger and held onto his father with his small hands, white knuckled, during snuggle time only releasing him when sleep finally, blessedly, won the fight.

Shane closed the bedroom door with barely a click, crossed across the living room on tip toes and collapsed on the secondhand futon that creaked under his weight.

The tower of bills stacked on the coffee table tottered dangerous on the edge. The grandfather clock, the only thing from his former life he hadn't sold, chimed one bell. He froze, fearing the sound would wake Kyle but, several seconds later and no sound from the boy's room, he released his breath. It was 11:30. A half hour before today officially melted into tomorrow.

"Midnight is the tipping point between the past and the future," Marcus would say back in the early days of their marriage. Shane smiled at the memory of his ex. The sound of his laugh, the way his eyebrows would crunch up when he read something stupid in the newspaper, the way he just was. Until one day, he just wasn't. The son of a bitch.

God, I need a break.

There was a joint D'Angelo and his latest fuckboy left as a housewarming present. Shane kept it hidden in a box crammed in the back of his sock drawer. That would take the edge off. Maybe, just a little. To help him to get to sleep.

He stood up, his heart a little lighter at the anticipation and then he crashed as reality slapped him back down. The interview. Dammit. What if they asked him to do a piss test?

Fuck.

He needed some way to take the edge off, something to relax him. He looked down at his crotch and bit his lip. *Maybe…* He leaned back, unzipped his fly, and rubbed his thumb over his cock, teasing it, waiting for that familiar tingle and rush but, no. Nothing. *Christ.* Not even masturbation stirred his interest.

Jesus, what a life.

He zipped up and walked into the darkened kitchen to make a cup of chamomile tea. Maybe it would help him at least get some sleep. The kitchen was small. A sink, a stove, a microwave that served more as a clock than anything else, and a fridge. There were three cabinets mounted to the wall and countertops that were a sickening pink and gray parquetry that always made Shane feel like he was in a John Waters' movie. The linoleum felt sticky and cold on his bare feet until he stepped on something hard that squished under the ball of his foot. He looked down to see a brown wrinkled raisin pop out of the backside of the roach. An egg sac. A goddamn egg sac.

"Fuckfuckfuckfuck." Shane muttered as he hopped on one foot to the counter and grabbled at the paper towel rack. The roll spun as the last sliver ripped off in a jagged strip. He choked down the vomit as he wiped the squished momma roach off his foot.

"Daddy?" The boy called out from his room.

Goddammit…can I have one damn minute to myself?

There was a crashing sound and, "DADDY!"

Shane dropped the crumbled-up paper towel and rushed

to his son like a shot.

"Kyle?"

The boy was sitting on the floor, near the opened closet, his legs splayed out in front of him.

I closed that door. I know I did. Kyle won't sleep with it open.

"Hey, buddy. Did you fall out of bed?"

The boy looked up and his eyes were blank, wide and wet. "Da..daa…daaaa," he said as his head slowly tilted to the right and his drooling mouth opened and closed erratically as if his jaw was snagged by wires.

Seizure! "I'm here, Kyle. Don't worry. Daddy's here."

Shane took two steps, reached down and the boy slid backwards, an inch closer to the closet.

"Kyle?" He took another step and the boy scooted backwards, again, just out of reach.

What the fuck?

Shane lifted a foot and Kyle was jerked to the left, smashing into the door jamb. The pain made the boy cry out and the sick blankness of his eyes lift.

"daddy….it hurts…."

"Oh, fuck this!" Shane rushed in, grabbed his son by the arms and pulled but and there was a quick, hard yank that threatened to drag the boy into the dark shadows of the closet.

"Let go!" Shane screamed into nothing and pulled the boy up to his chest.

The light came back to Kyle's eyes and he started bawling. "Don't let me go, Daddy!"

"It's okay. I got you, buddy." He brushed back the boy's hair, pulling strands away from the snot and tears running down his face. "Everything will be okay."

Shane felt another tug, like a fish on a line.

Kyle grabbed his father tighter, his little fingers digging into Shane's neck. "Stop it! Make it stop, Daddy…it burns!"

Shane looked down to see a veiny rope, so very thin as to be like a spider's web, wrapped around Kyle's waist. It was slimy and where it touched the skin, tarry lines spread out like fingers up the spine. He had seen something like that when a kid he knew was bitten by a spider. The venom radiated outwards from the bite, the poison turning the veins into a roadmap.

What the fuck?

Moonlight streamed through the window enough so he could follow the glistening line as it wavered in midair and disappeared into the dark, dark closet. The line trembled as it pulled taunt, grew slack and grew taunt again as if it were breathing.

He plucked it like a guitar string.

Thwang.

A second later, an answer.

Ping.

Kyle whimpered.

Ping.

"Daddy! It hurts!"

Ping.

"What the hell?"

Pingpingpingping.

With each ping, Kyle screamed like a crazed animal and kicked viciously into Shane's thighs.

"Stop, Kyle! I'm going to drop you! Stop!"

Shane hooked a finger around the line and tried to snap it. "Holy shit!" he yelled as the line burned his finger, leaving a painful white welt.

"*Shhhhhh,*" said a voice from the closet. It was a wet, globby sound as if someone was drowning in mucous. "*Quiet, quiet, quiet now. Mustn't scare away the tasty.*"

The line tugged on the boy and he cried out in pain. Shane moved in to relieve the pressure on Kyle.

"*So close….close, close, close NOW!*"

A jerk strong enough to pull Shane off his feet slammed him to his knees and yanked Kyle out of his arms.

"DADDY!" Kyle screamed as he was dragged away.

"Kyle!' Shane scrambled to all fours. Kyle's feet and legs were already inside and it was only seconds before he would be consumed completely. He leaped forward, snagging the collar on the boy's pajamas with his fingertips. "I got you, buddy!" He could feel the cheap fabric starting to rip as he pulled against whatever force had him from the other side. He wrestled with the shirt until he had a firmer grip on the boy's shoulders. "I got you!" He flipped himself around, pulling Kyle up towards his chest and dragged the boy out, inches at a time until whatever was in the darkness pulled back, harder, dragging Shane and Kyle towards the door. "Shit!" The cheap carpet scraped his back as he was pulled towards the closet. He put his feet up and caught the door jamb. The sudden stop made his ankles pop with the strain as the force within kept on with the battle.

"The tasty, the tasty, the TASTY!!"

"Daddy! It's biting me! Ow, ow, ow! DaadDDY!"

Kyle wriggled in his arms and cried out in pain as Shane felt his ankles shake with the strain.

There was a tug and then slack.

They were at a stalemate.

"Let go, you son of a bitch! Let go!"

"No, no, no. YOU let go of the tasty. Let it go and be free."

"What?"

Kyle lifted his head. His eyes were dull, grayish orbs and his lips open and closed, like a gasping fish. Shane felt a warm rush as the boy's bladder released.

"Give the tasty to me. Be free." The words poured from his lips. *"I will pluck it out from your world. Erase it. Snip snap. No more. Memories, snip snaps, snip snaps, snip snaps of brain dreams. Your world. Blessed with snip snaps. Easy, easy, easy. Give the tasty and I can snip snap that away from the world, from you too. See, see, see?"*

Kyle reached out and planted his small palm on Shane's forehead. Memories of his life before fatherhood played out like a montage in searing, unbelievable colors. Expensive tailored shirts and expense accounts. A thriving business and a future paved in success. The days before sweatpants hid his thickening dad-bod. Back then, there were lazy days at the beach. Restaurants. Laughing, drinking, and dancing at the club with beautiful friends. A lifetime ago when he felt young, exciting, and sexy. The future was open and free. More memories. Of Marcus. Goddamn it. Marcus smiling. Marcus driving down to Laguna Beach with the top down. Marcus…Marcus…Marcus…

Shame and regret burned in his face as tears blinded his sight. "That's not fair."

"All yours, all yours, all back to you. Erase the tasty, I will. Snip snap, Your world forgets. Soon, you even forget." It tugged at the line and Kyle slipped, just a little, until Shane's grip tightened. The boy's lips quivered as the thick, sloppy words poured out of his mouth. *"Give me the tasty."*

God, I'm so tired.

The grandfather clock chimed. Midnight. The tipping point between today and tomorrow. The past and the future.

Marcus.

He took the easy way out. The bastard.

And I'm so damn tired.

The throbbing in his ankles were like lightning bolts surging through his legs. They shook under the pressure of holding them from the precipice. His arms felt heavy and he grunted as he fought to keep a grip on Kyle.

"Let me go…daddy." The last word was forced from his son's lips. As if it were a foreign, unheard word spoken by an alien. *"I want to go. I need to go."*

The tugging increased and Shane pulled back. "No! Fuck you!"

Kyle's head reared back until his gray dead orbs glared at him as he growled, *"Let. The. TAAAASTY. GO!"* The boy bared his teeth and clamped down on Shane's bicep with such force a baby tooth lodged into his skin.

Shane screamed in pain and anger. The boy bit deeper and shook his head like a dog with a chew toy. The muscle in his arm was shredding and he could feel the strength draining away. The baby tooth ripped out and fell to the floor with a quiet plink. "Kyle! Jesus, help me! Kyle, listen to me, awwwgawd!" He set his jaw against the pain and hugged the boy closer, pulling the chomping mouth out of his arm. Blood flowed down his arm and out of his son's mouth. "I told you that I will never let you go. I have your back, Buddy. For now and for always!"

With the last remaining ounce of strength in his body, Shane rolled over, pressing the boy beneath him. He kicked at the line, wrapping it around his calf and prayed the pants leg would protect him from the burning. It did. He rolled over once more causing Kyle to grunt and go limp. Shane saw the line break from around his son and begin to slither away, uncurling around his leg.

"Oh, no, you motherfucker. You don't get away that easy." He turned his leg and twisted the remaining line tighter than then PULLLLLLLED-

There was resistance.

"Come out..." Shane growled through clenched teeth.

"Nooo, noo.....uuuuh.....no fight...no tasty.....let go...letgoletgolet-go..."

"You fucker.....come out and fight me...NOW!" and with

his left leg he pushed against the floor, scooting backwards as he pulled violently with the right leg.

Then a sound like a cannonball expelled from a thick wall of gelatin, a squishy, wet sound and then a thud as something landed on the floor.

It looked like an old woman, frail and thin, covered in clear slime, lying face down. Her hair trailed down her back in thick plaits that ended at her hips, beyond that were squamous tentacle like strands of snot and rot. She pushed up on her spidery arms and raised her small head. Her face was long and skeleton, gaping holes for eyes, a flat blank space for a nose. Her mouth was a decaying hole where black shards passed for teeth. From that cancerous orifice, Shane could see the beginning of gelatinous fishing line that was wrapped around his leg.

"Holy fucking Christ, what are you?" he cried out in disgust and crabwalked further away, grasping the unconscious Kyle closer to his chest.

The line neatly unwrapped from around Shane's leg as the creature cocked her head back and reeled the line into her mouth with a nauseating slurping sound. Finished, she smiled and made a purring sound as she slithered into the darkness of the closet.

"Bye, bye, my taaasty." And it winked.

"Oh, fuck no. You aren't going anywhere, bitch," said Shane as he rolled Kyle off his chest. He went to the toy chest and pulled out a baseball bat and started to follow her…*it*…into the closet.

"Daddy?" Kyle whimpered.

Shane stopped at the sound of his name and went back to his son as the thing disappeared into the darkness.

Shane stared into the closet at the darkness within.

Phlegmatic laughter bubbled from the darkness.

"Oh, hell…oh fuck no." Shane slammed the closet door shut, pushed the chest of drawers against and then slid down to the floor, collapsing in front of this blockade of cheap plywood and discount furniture.

Kyle crawled over into his father's lap. His ankles were bleeding and his pajama bottoms were wet with piss. The boy shuddered in the chill. "Is it gone, Daddy? Are we safe now?"

Shane looked down into his desperate son's eyes. What could he tell him? What should he tell him? That sometimes the monsters win? That sometimes there is nothing you can do to hold off the monster with teeth and claws as it tears down the walls, rips you apart, consumes you until you're expelled in a diarrheic spurt? That there were monsters in the world and that sometimes all you had was each other? Forever and ever?

What could he say?

Shane smiled, put up a fist and waited for Kyle to bump it.

"Forever and ever, buddy. You and me."

The End

THE CLEANER

35

For APS

Good morning! Have a good night's sleep? I had a rough night here, wooo-boy, let me tell ya…what? Oh, where's the house? It…well, it burned down.

Whoa, whoa, whoa! Calm down! I didn't intend for all this to happen, believe you me. I didn't come here last night thinking, 'Whoa Nelly! What this place needs is a C-4 enema!' So, just stow your cellphone, there's no need to call the police. They were here already with the fire department. And don't even bother calling your lawyer. All of this was covered in the "incidents beyond and above the Cleaner's control" clause in the contract you signed before you hired me. I swear, I tried my best but frankly, my friend, there wasn't much that could be done for this house. It was Bad, plain and simple.

How? Look, houses ain't just made up of wood and iron nails, slab concrete and copper pipes. They are more than that. As far back as when they was just animal hides stretched over tent poles and right on up to them Mcmansions of nowadays, they have always been more than just *that*. They hover over us like mothers, their backs shielding us as we stay safe inside their bellies, living our lives. All of our pain and our happiness, all those stories boiling and rolling inside their walls, how could you not expect them to take us in and absorb some of that life?

And some of the stuff this poor old girl has seen… whooo-boy. Nasty.

Don't believe me? Just look down any street. See that house over there? The one with the white gingerbread lattice work and the freshly painted red door? See the golden, satisfied glow coming from its windows? That house is *loved*, my friend, it is happy, like a fat Persian cat after a bowl of primo catnip.

Now, take a look at that house across the street. See how

it faces north, always in the shadow? Look up there. See how the roof slumps like a swayback horse? You can feel the cold that pours off it. It's not just the aesthetics that chill your bones. Hell, I've been inside houses where the damn floor was caving in right under your feet but it still felt warm and alive. That house there is like a beaten dog. A dog comes into this world ready to give love, loyalty and protection, with no second thoughts.

It's the same way for a house. Only, sometimes it doesn't turn out that way.

Let me try to explain it to you in simple terms: Rentals like this are the whores of the real estate world.   A rented house is used, uncared for. People come in, go out, come in and go out, leaving behind a stain of sweat and sin. No one expects to stay long. They unpack their boxes and leave their garbage wadded up in the corner and then they leave. The owner drops by, slaps on a thin veneer of paint to cover the brown tracks on the walls and slaps another plastic coated "FOR RENT" sign in the window. "SEE OWNER FOR DETAILS".

She's a whore. Plain and simple.

And that's what brings us to your problem, dunnit?

Now, don't tell me, let me guess. It all started with just a feeling, like this suffocating pressure, a balloon that keeps getting bigger and bigger until the skin is stretched so thin that it finally POPS!, leaving your ears ringing.

But that's just the beginning.

What happened next? Smells? Or did you start hearing voices? Looking at your face, I bet it was the voices that got to you next. Men don't care much about smells; they just laugh 'em off. But voices, now, that scares a man. Too solid to laugh off, ain't it. Did they call your name? Or were they screaming? Maybe from the fire?

You didn't know about that? Caveat emptor, my friend.

You bought this place cheap. Probably at some property tax sale, pennies to the dollar. I keep up with real estate gossip; it's my bread and butter. According to what I hear, this section of town is due for some gentrification. Soon, we'll be up to our balls in yuppies and guppies looking for a cheap "historic" home to gut and make their own. I bet when you found this honey for sale, you thought you were getting a sweet deal. You figure you'd swoop down here, do some fast renovations and flip it for a nice profit.

It's a good plan except you never counted on all this hammering stirring up a whole mess of trouble.

See, what you are doing here, it's sort of like tearing off a bandage from a wound that ain't never been properly healed. The scab that was keeping everything down done come clean off and all that stuff underneath, it starts to ooze out.

And that's when you get troubles, my friend. And that's why you called me.

There's always been one or two of us, going back generations. When we were still back up in the mountains, they called us 'layers' because we could be called on to 'lay down spirits'. Nowadays, that term doesn't have quite the same meaning. I prefer to call myself a Cleaner. It sounds more respectable.

Back then, all a layer needed to do to get the job done was throw around a cup of rock salt or burn a bundle of sage, smudge the whole damn house. I always thought that was for show, to tell the truth, I ain't never needed no herbs to see what I sees. Still, they were simpler jobs in those days, I bet. It was just laying down relatives that didn't want to move on. People stayed put in those days. One house, one family. Nothing too complicated in that.

Now, with all this coming and going, the most used tool I have is in my wallet: my library card. It's amazing all the stuff you can learn if you just sit down a spell and open a goddamn book.

You bought quite a piece of history, my friend.

Here's a folder full of clippings I found in the archives. You can keep it; I've already put it on my bill. Looks like there's been a few murders, a suicide and that's just what made the papers. I'm sure there's a few stories this house could tell that were never heard outside these walls.

Like how all this land here used to be a county farm that housed the poor and the mentally ill. Back at the turn of the century, both were considered nearly the same. Most of the farm burned down mysteriously in the winter of 1910. From what I can find out, this house here, well… the one that was here anyway… was one of the few that survived the fire. After the smoke cleared, others on the farm began to wonder why it was their houses that burned while this one still stood. Lots of bad talk got started and with the cold coming on, the ones left with nowhere to go decided that the fortunate few should share their good luck. However, the Haves tend to see things a little differently than the Have Nots and, as history has shown, when these two forces clash, very little good tends to come to either party.

In the folder is a copy of the court records from the trial in 1910. It was quite the scandal back in the day when John Q. Public wasn't so callous to murders by the dozen, even if it was just a bunch of poor Irish and a pack of crazies.

I couldn't find any records of who took ownership directly after the fire. Since it was County property, I figure it probably stood vacant until it went up for auction and some poor fool bought it probably much like you did.

The first deed I found was in 1942 to a Leland Beck. His family was big in real estate and added most of the houses left behind by the fire to their stable. It's all there in the folder. And, just for flavor, take a peek at the police reports I was able to match up to the houses on that list. Oh, yes, my friend, you bought into a very nasty piece of history.

Which brings us to last night.

It didn't take much. When I got here, I could feel it was ready to blow. The skin of that bubble was pulled painfully tight, coming so thin at places you could hear the squeal of the air squeezing out. For some cases, this is as far as it would go, like a battery, charging down. Eventually, all this would just die down on its own since most people don't give off enough spark to complete the circuit, so to speak. However, people like me, we tend to be sparkier than others. In this instance, I was damn near a Roman candle.

I won't take up your time, telling you all I saw, all the horrors I felt ripping through me when it all broke. Read the file. You can understand all you need to know.

I'm sorry the house burnt but, seeing the history, you don't need me to foresee why it came to pass. I sympathize with your loss but there wasn't nothing that could be done for this place. It wasn't a normal laying, no sir, there weren't nothing here to lay! Nothing human, no ways. More like a festering psychic boil that had to be lanced, letting the poison run out until it was done. Even if you don't believe in a place being cursed, you can still hold to a place being wrong. And this house was Wrong. Bad Wrong.

But it's done now, all of it. Here's the reports from the fire department and the police; your insurance company should be able to do the rest. I salted the ground, did a little special mojo of my own so you shouldn't be having any more problems. The land is cleared so you can build yourself something new. Just keep in mind what I told you about houses being more than bricks and pipes and you'll be fine.

Now, if you'll excuse me, the people across the street have just come home and I think I see someone who needs my business card.

The End

REGINALD

For Natural Born Freaks Everywhere

Reginald's mother wrung her hands into a knot as she tried to explain to the First Baptist Women's Auxiliary that her Reginald was not a drug addict like you see on the TV, hanging out over in San Francisco. This was Oklahoma, for God's sake, not Haight-Ashbury. Her Reginald was a free spirit, a poet, she told the squinty eyed old women visiting after the Sunday sermon, nothing more.

"We know about the cow, Melvina." Miss Odella Grunch, the pastor's sister was the tallest of the five. A spinster by nature, it was said that she did not cry at her birth but smirked and slapped at the doctor's hand cradling her naked, shriveled rear end. She had that same sly grin on her face right now as she watched Melvina flinch. The other four nodded and circled around Odella like a murder of crows, their prim black dresses creating a pool of inky shadow. "And we know about what he did at the courthouse. Alma's girl, Fleur, sits next to Bethany whose mother is a file clerk at the courthouse."

 Fleur's mother, a chubby little woman, chirped up. "She saw the marriage license and everything. My girl told me everything, she did."

"What?" Melvina choked out, her throat felt like it was becoming tighter and tighter. She turned to face Jim, her husband, who sat shielded behind his newspaper fort. He ruffled the pages as he felt her eyes burning into the newsprint. She turned back to the women. "What in Heaven's name are you talking about? A *cow? Are you saying my boy-?* "

"Up and married a cow, Melvina."

"Oh, my sweet boy. No!" Melvina said as she started to swoon. Odella swooped over and embraced Melvina and, tucking her under one arm, walked her over to the couch. The black brood followed them.

"We aren't here to judge." Odella said. The clutch of old women shook their heads vigorously. "No one here can do that, Sweet God knows. Still, we all should've seen this coming, really. It was inevitable. First, it was with the homosexuals and now, well, with all the new breeds coming in all the time."

"It's all that foul science over at the Hill Institute!" Glynnis, a short, toothless woman trumpeted, "It's unnatural! Against the will of God, it is!"

"I won't have you saying a word against that Institute. "Fleur's mother said, her face growing red. "If it wasn't for them, I wouldn't have my little Fleur."

"*Fleur.*" Glynnis spit out the name. "More like *Fur.* What did they mix you up with anyway? Tomcat? That would explain a lot about your little *Fleur.*"

Odella Grunch stood up and spread out her arms, her dark cloak falling like black wings, "Women!" she screeched. "We will not squabble and peck each other to death! Everyone in this town owes a great debt to the Institute."

"I don't." smirked Glynnis, snapping her toothless gums, "They came along, way after I was born. Never done nothing for me or mine."

Odella turned on the old woman, who cowered beneath her. "Your sort could never afford Dr. Morff treatments and that's the brutal end of it, Glynnis. Why else did you all let your boy, Benny, die?"

The old woman's eyes hardened, and she thrust her chin out until they stood nose to hooked nose.

"Mine ain't never come up short for nothing, you dried up old crow. We might not have much, but we are all natural. My boy died complete, nothing taken, nothing transformed. Straight up human to the core. And that's something all your shiny things can never buy." Glynnis hobbled away, slamming the door behind her.

"Well." Odella said, stroking her crest of hair down. "Wasn't that illuminating? I think we shall take our leave now, Melvina. We only meant to come and visit and pass on the news. We'll see you at chorus practice on Wednesday?"

Melvina nodded and stood up to escort her guests out.

"No need, dear. We'll all make our way out ourselves." And with a flurry of goodbyes, they were gone.

Melvina ran back to the kitchen to where her husband Jim like to sit and relax before Sunday dinner.

"Jim!" she said through her sobs. "Did you hear that? Reginald has gone off. He left us. With a cow!"

Jim gently folded his newspaper and, swatting at the pesky flies that hovered around him, went over to his wife. He gently nudged her with is long muzzle. "It could've been worse, Mellie. Could've been a pig."

The End

THE

UNANSWERED

CALL

For Alan

January, 13, 1935. Friday.

I fell hard inside the phone booth, keeping my hand squeezed up against my guts. It was the only thing keeping them where they belonged.

"Operator. 5551879. Reverse the charges."

The ringing clanged inside my skull. I shook my head as my vision began to tunnel. The vertigo brought me back in time to hear the click of the connection.

"James?"

"Ricky!! Sweetie, where have you been?"

Doris. Just my rotten luck. "Doll, put James on."

She hummed along to some stupid song that was playing in the background. "I've missed you, sweetie."

Christ. "Get James. Do you hear me? Get him now!"

"He's not here, handsome. But I'm here, all alone."

I leaned against the phone. The cool metal kissed my swollen jaw. "Where is he?"

"I don't know and I don't much care!" She clicked her tongue. Jesus, what piece of work. It didn't take much for me to imagine her lower lip quiver as she pouted and stamped her size 5 champagne pink stilettos. My partner, James, was dizzy for the dame but, to me, she was dust. "James is such a grouch. He packed a bag and split right after you left." I heard her gasp. "Oh…God. Ricky, do you think he knows?"

Not this mess again. One sloppy New Year's romp and this bird pegged us for the next Bogie and Bacall. "Don't be loopy. There's nothing to know so stop bumping your gums about it.”

“Don’t be that way, Ricky. I’m lonely. I need you-“

“Not as much as I need James. Find him. Tell him I am at Percy’s at 555-1478. Sing that back to me. Good.”

“Rick-!”

I hung up before her voice drilled me another hole and sat down on the wooden seat. Warmth flooded over my hands. I closed the door with my foot. The winter damp was beginning to creep into my shoes. The Nashville Arcade was empty. Not a pigeon in sight. Beside the phone booth, Percy’s Shoe Shine Shop was dark. It was strange seeing it so hollow. It looked lifeless without the hustle of suits waiting for their shines.

Outside the Arcade, Fifth Avenue was quiet. Maybe the goons hadn’t followed me. Maybe they had given up. Or maybe they were just a block over in Printer’s Alley waiting for me to surface like a rat from the gutter. Either way, no reason to get hinky with an ambulance siren. I’ll just wait it out for James.

Where was he?

He had sent me on a box job. A simple can opener, nothing fancy. Crack the safe, get the goods and get out. A clean sneak. James owed an old friend a favor, he’d said. He passed it on to me because-

“You got the touch, Priest. The tumblers just fall underneath your fingers, don’t they, pal?”

I never got to find out. I was copped before I laid finger one on the box. Palookas sapped me on the conk. I came to tied to a chair with two lugs using my mug for batting practice. A double breasted bull polished his badge while he asked me where I'd hidden the stash, who had hired me to steal it. Nobody wanted to hear my patsy sob song. The bull worked me over good and played my ribcage like a xylophone. I tasted copper long before he finished his first scale.

Lucky for me, his thugs weren't boy scouts. Their knots were weak. At the first sign of an intermission in their fist concerto, I made a break.

I didn't see the gun but I felt the bullets all the same. They drilled straight through my back and out my gut.

I ran through the streets until I made it to the Arcade, to the phone booth besides Percy's. James knows this place. We get our shoes shined for a nickel here. We act sweet to the girls down at the Peanut Shop and get free bags of hot nuts. He knows where to find me, knows where to call me. If only that dingbat can find him in time.

James, what the hell was in that safe?

So many questions. How did such a simple gig go south so fast? James said he cased the joint for a week. It was supposed to be empty. I barely got my nose in the door before they swooped down on me like so many crows.

'The tumblers just fall underneath your fingers, don't they, pal?'

I felt a cold stab in my kidneys. I coughed and spit up blood. The echoes of a deep, slow beat came towards me from a long tunnel. My head swimmed with the idea.

He packed a bag and split right after you left.

Dammit. My head is spinning.

God, I'd kill for a deck of Luckies. My lungs are aching for a drag. Then, I could think straight. Not be getting my guts wadded in my garters thinking up crazy Chinese angles like James hanging me out to dry. He'll call. The phone will ring, anytime now.

What if-

No…don't even start down that line. He doesn't know anything because there's nothing to know! Break it up… stop right there. We're like brothers, James and me. We drink from the same bottle. We're on the square. He'd never send me to get bumped off by a couple of Brunos. He'd never just lam off and leave me…

But-

Just ring, damn you! Ring!

James knows. Dammit, he knows.

I'll call Chesty. Sure. Chesty. He just lives over the bridge, owes me a fin from last week's card game. He'll come and we'll call it even steven. Everything will be golden.

But…I can't reach the phone.

My arm, my legs. Feels like I'm coated in cold lead. My gut. There is more blood than shirt now. So cold…so cold. I can't move. Have I frozen stiff? Can that happen so fast? No, don't be a galook. No, it's not…not…that. Tired. I'm just tired. That's all. I can barely see. Are my eyes open?

Make the call. I can't.

Just…reach.

He knows.   Sweet Jesus, James knows.

                oh god………help me.   Why won't the phone ring? Please. Just…

James   i'm   didn't   mean

                                          i   am

January 13. Today.

BRRRRRRNG! BRRRRRRNG!

"What the hell?!?" Terrance Donaldson looked down at the man shining his shoes. "What was that?"

Kel looked up at the young man sitting high in what his daddy used to call 'the Businessman's Throne'. "What's that, sir?"

BRRRRRRNG! BRRRRRRNG!

"Didn't you hear that? It was like an old timey telephone ringing right next to my ear. I nearly spilled my latte!" Terrance pulled his Blackberry out of his jacket pocket and shrugged. "Sometimes my kid changes my ringtone to mess with me."

Kel rolled an eye over to Chester, a shoe shiner who had worked in Percy's since Noah set down his ark. "Did you hear anything, old man?"

Chester sat in an empty chair as he waited for another lunch hour middle management stooge to blow in from the Arcade. He kept his eyes on the television as he rolled an unlit cigar in his mouth and silently cursed the new no smoking laws. "It ain't nothing to worry about, mister." he said. "It's been doing that since Kel's daddy's time. Don't know where it comes from."

"That's just crazy. There has to be a reason."

Chester shrugged. "We mostly just ignore it."

"Maybe a phone upstairs is echoing down through the vents?"

Kel shook his head. "My daddy said there used to be an old phone booth he swore was haunted. He told me stories of how Chester and my granddaddy used to tell the kids that if you answered the phone, the devil would snatch you up. City tore it down back in the fifties. There's an ATM there now. "

He did a last swipe at the young man's leather shoes. "There you go, sir. That will be 5 dollars."

The young man handed him a ten dollar bill. "Keep the change. Thanks for the story, guys. I'll have something to talk about back at the office."

"Thank you, sir. Hope to see you soon. Tell your friends." Kel smiled as he pocketed the money.

Chester gave a slight nod to the young man as he left. He rolled the cigar around in his mouth and grimaced. Some days, the shadow of the taste was enough but not today. He took it out of his mouth and looked longingly at the unlit tip. It was on slow, melancholy days like this he could feel the sour frustration in the ringing phone, the need to make that final connection. It was a cross only the old understand. He looked down again, longing for the warmth of smoke in his lungs. The unlit cigar. The unanswered call.

The End

WHAT THE ARMLESS GUY SAID

57

For Richard, who always believed

My name is Travis Dare and the Great Outdoors can kiss my psychic ass.

I don't like sleeping on rocks or squatting over tree roots to take a dump. It's either too hot or too cold. Too wet or I'm covered in goddamn bugs. I prefer worldly comforts like a toilet and being able to control my environment with the flip of a switch. Call me evolved.

And yet here I am, in Oregon, setting up camp for a dead man.

At least today is a comfortable 70 degrees. You would never have guessed that, six months ago, this entire region was neck deep in snow.

Or that a man froze to death, right over there.

His name was Tobias Ellison. Maybe you remember him. It was all over the news. He, his wife, Lacie, and the twins, Robin and Echo were on the way to visit family for Christmas. They took a wrong turn and ended up stranded. After three days, Tobias left to get help. Two days later, rescuers tracked down the car using GPS pings or some kind of tech wizardry. The family was scared, cold but at least they were now safe.

It took another three days before they found Tobias' frozen carcass.

His friends and family consoled themselves with how brave and selfless he was to go out into the blizzard with no thoughts for his own safety. He risked and lost all for his family. All the talking heads on TV labeled him a hero. It was a tragic Christmas news story. The media ate it up.

Between you and me, my ass would have stayed put. Cars are much easier to spot than some idiot climbing over a snow covered mountain. But, hey, that's just me. I'm no hero.

But here I am, in a borrowed tent, drinking my last beer, waiting for one.

****

The park ranger was surprised that I wanted to set up camp in this spot. "Nobody likes it here," he said. "It's got a weird vibe. Even the bird watchers have complained that the birds have stopped coming through here."

"Well, I like it weird."

I might have given him a bad first impression.

After three matches and scorched fingertips, I got a campfire going and put on some coffee. I didn't have to wait very long; these things usually find me. I'm lucky that way.

At first, it was big balls of light that weaved through the trees. I watched a glowing blob, the biggest of the bunch, as it bounced around, and elongated into the shape of a man. My head started to get that heavy feeling, the kind I get right before a migraine hits. A tickling burning sensation started, right on the edge of my fingertips, and slowly turned into stream of electricity that shot up my arms and made the hairs stand up.

"*Showtime*," I said under my breath.

Then I saw him. He stood at the edge of the trees and stared at the fire, confused and slack-jawed. His arms were wrapped tight around his chest and he shivered violently to fight off the cold in spite of the July heat. He was wearing a t-shirt under a stylishly faded denim jacket, a pair of jeans and high top Converse shoes. His shoulder length black hair was frozen to his pale cheeks. He looked like the photos that were splashed all over the newspapers covering the tragedy, except that he was missing his ret-ro-chic Buddy Holly glasses. Interesting fact: I have never seen a ghost wearing eyeglasses, my hand to God. I can't figure it out. Why go through the trouble of manifesting jeans and sneakers but then blow off the glasses?

"Tobias!" I called out to him.

He heard me. That's a good sign. Maybe he's not too far gone.

"Come on over here, closer to the fire. Warm yourself up."

He took a step towards me but then stopped. He wavered, staggering as if hearing something over his shoulder, and then he wandered away into the tree line.

Dammit, we've got a runner.

Well, it's not so much running. It's really more of a mean-der, really. If I'm lucky, he'll stay on course. I really hate it when they start popping in and out, zig zagging all over the place, like a hard shelled bug slamming up against the porch light. Not only did it set off my vertigo, it's creepy as hell.

I caught up to him. "TOBIAS!" I shouted, trying to get his attention.

He stopped but doesn't turn to face me. I don't want to touch him; ghosts leave me feeling numb and slightly nauseous. I can't explain it. Maybe it's some sort of EMF thing.

He started to fade. Dammit, if I lose him, I'll have to spend another night out here in Bigfoot country. I pulled out my ace in the hole, "Tobias Ellison! I know where your family is."

That got his attention. He thickened. It's the easiest way to explain it. He just became more *there*. He turned and his eyes focused on me for the first time.

"Wh-where are th-th-they?" he said. His voice stuttered from cold and desperation. "I c-c-can't find th-them."

"Follow me," I said.

He stumbled over to the fire clumsily, as if his legs were frozen solid. He stood close and the air grew colder as if he had brought his own pocket of December with him.

"I brewed some coffee," I said, pouring out a cup. "It's awful but it's hot."

He ignored me and looked into the fire. He's already forgotten that I was even there. You have to work hard to keep ghosts on track; their minds wander like a fart in the wind.

"Hey!" I said sharply. His eyes were lost, gray and filmy. "Here. Take this cup of coffee. It'll warm you up."

He took the cup and drank from it. I don't know how this is physically possible. It's something I don't think too hard about . My guess is that humans won't let something like being incorporeal get in the way of a good, stiff drink. Like the armless guy said, 'Where there is a will, there is a way.'

"My…..car…." he said slowly, his icy lips barely able to form the words. "My family….in the car….so cold… can't find them. Where are they?"

"They aren't here." I take a drink from my cup, happy that my coffee has whiskey in it. "They were rescued, two days after you went walking, They are all home, safe and warm."

"But… I just left them…they were…just here." He dropped the cup and slowly turned away.

"NO!" I said with a little more force than needed and my voice nailed him solid. I'm sorry to sound like a har-dass but, sometimes, you really have to whack these guys upside the head to keep them focused. Ghosts are stupid like that.

"Come here. Sit down."

He sat down, falling like a load of laundry. He shivered more violently now than ever. I tossed the remains of my cup into the fire, the flames flared from the alcohol. He didn't react at all. I was losing him again. I reached into my backpack and pulled out a newspaper that had all the details of the rescue of his family. "Here. Read this. Maybe it will help you to get a grip on things."

He took the paper and stared at the headline. His face was flat and dull. Turning the paper over, he looked at a picture of himself with his two little girls. He flipped the paper back to the headline, "Missing Father Found-Tragic End" to the photo several times, each turn shorter than the last. I could see the connectors firing but I didn't think we had an arc yet.

"Maybe this will clear things up." I pulled out another newspaper. The headlines on this one read "Heroic Dad Found Frozen on Bear Creek Road". I tossed it over to him and, remarkably, he caught it. Good reflexes for a dead guy. Did caffeine work on the dead? I know that sometimes it's the only thing keeping me moving.

He read it once, just once, and threw it into the fire. The slick, gray film faded away and his eyes were clear and sharp, like a perfectly focused camera.

"I'm dead." He said it, just like that. No question. Just a blanket statement.

"Yeah, sorry, but you went out a hero."

"BULLSHIT!" he said, kicking the fire. The kick actually managed to push a few of the sticks and red orange embers soared up with the heat. His face was twisted in frustration.

"Whoa! Settle down. Talk to me, kid." I said. "What's wrong?"

"It's all wrong. All of it. It wasn't like that. I mean…what the papers said…what you think." He kept his eyes on the fire. He chewed on his lower lip, unable to look at me. "I'm…not anything like that at all." He stood up so forcefully that he floated for a second by the fire. "Tell me…how does someone in the 21st century get lost in the fucking mountains? Huh? Explain that to me!"

I shrugged. "So, what's your story? Why did you leave the car?"

"Man, I don't know." He ran his hands through his wet hair in frustration. "I just couldn't take it anymore. The crying. The bitching. Oh God! The bitching! Lacie kept riding my ass about how if we'd only had gone to her mom's house in San Diego we'd be on a beach right now and how if I'd gotten the GPS system for the trip instead of the DVD player for the kids, everything would've been okay. Then, to top it all off, the kids got sick. One was barfing while the other was shitting a river. We ran out of diapers fast. Lacie kept on me, like it was my fault and… well, I couldn't take it anymore. I needed some air, ya know."

"So, you just went walking? Where the hell did you think you would go?"

"I know, I know! I'm a dumbass, all right?!? I didn't plan on going far. I was just going to walk around a little. Get out and clear my head."

For the first time, I see the ghost-hero for what he is: a young, selfish, stupid kid in way over his head. All those reporters on the news pegged him Father of the Year. I guess, with it being Christmas, a hero was good for ratings.

I shook my head and laugh. "Sounds like Mr. Hero wasn't thinking at all."

"You think you're funny? You think *this* is funny? I'm dead, asshole! I'm only 23! It's not fair! I've got a family to take care of. My mom…my dad. Oh, God, I screwed everything up. And you think this is funny?!"

I held my hands up. "Sorry. But it's over. You're dead and there's no going back. Now comes the big question: what are you going to do now?"

"I don't know." He slumped down and bit his lip again. "What should I do? Are you an angel? Here to show me the way to…" he waved his hands over his head, "… wherever?"

"I'm no angel. Sorry, kid. I come from a family of what the old timers called 'ghost layers'. We help the dead who for whatever reason have a hard time crossing over. As a matter of fact, you might call me the B Team. My grandmother is the heavy hitter. She is usually the one tagged by the Powers That Be for things like this but she is out on a cruise with her dart club."

"Great. Even in death I get shafted with the B team."

"I figured this would be an easy job. I had you pegged as being one of those 'Oh my God, I'm dead!' ghosts and, pop!, you'd cross right over to the Other Side. So, just work with me, okay? Damn. You think I want to be here?"

"Sorry."

"So, you don't see anything? No shining shaft of white light? No Grandma waving you over?"

"My grandmother is still alive." he said, smirking. "Some psychic you are."

"You know what I mean, dumbass."

He shook his head. "I don't feel cold anymore. That's got to be a good sign, right?" He clenched and unclenched his fist and wriggled his fingers as if it were the first time. "It is weird. I don't *feel* anything."

"You shouldn't feel anything. Nothing physical, anyway. That's one of the big benefits of being incorporeal. You felt cold before because you *thought* you were cold. The only reason you even look the way you do is because this is how you see yourself. Look, here's a quick primer in Ghost 101. You are no longer hampered by a body and all the crap that comes with the physical plane. Intention and Will are the two biggest factors in your life, as it is. If you want to go somewhere, you just think it and POP! there you are."

"This is awesome!" He glows a little brighter. "I feel like I can go anywhere, do anything."

"Wherever your heart desires."

"I want to go to Paris. Or the moon! Can I go to the

moon?"

I nodded. "Sure. But don't dawdle. It's not healthy for spirits to stay on this plane for very long."

"Why not?"

"That rush you're feeling? It won't last. You'll need to recharge by siphoning off psychic energy from living people and, trust me, it can get really messy. Ask my ex."

"So, how do I cross over?"

"The question I have is why haven't you? My guess is unresolved issues. Guilt. Worry. All the regular tropes."

"Lacie. The kids. Leaving them." His glow dims and his eyes glazed over. "I hate myself for that."

"Sounds like a good bet."

"I need to say goodbye. Make sure they are okay." The idea perked him up. "To get home, all I have to do is focus on my wife and kids and I should just, POP, be there, right?"

"Yes. Home, the moon, Paris, anywhere."

"And I could make it up to them. For leaving. And fighting with Lacie...everything." He looked thoughtful for a moment and then his smile faded. "What if they don't want me? What if I missed my chance?"

"Hey, they think you're a hero. I won't tell anyone you're an asshole. The secret is safe with me."

He laughed. I don't normally like it when ghosts laugh. It's a creepy sound, too echoey and hollow. But this is a good laugh, from his heart. He held out his hand as if to shake mine. I reciprocated although my hand will feel frostbitten for hours.

"So, tell me, I'm curious. Where are you going first?"

"Only one place. Home."

And he vanished.

I lifted up my empty cup in salute. "Amen, brother. Amen."

The End

THUMB DRIVE

For Beth G.

Please. Turn off your phone. No, no. Don't just put it away. Didn't you hear me? I said to turn it off. TURN. IT. OFF. No…no…please don't….don't call security. I know…I know…how I look…I look…I wasn't always this way.

You laugh. Don't laugh at me.

You don't know. YOU. DON'T. FUCKING. KNOW!!

Sorry, sorry…..I didn't mean to touch you….please. Don't call security…I promise…I promise I'll keep my distance. Just listen..to my story…just listen, will you?

It was a few years ago. I was home, working. I was always working back then. Accounting, spreadsheets. They were my world, back then. I heard someone fumbling outside the door, a loud curse and then the click of the deadbolt unlatching. I started to look up but remembered that it wouldn't be Lanie, so I kept my head buried in my spreadsheets.

It was Lanie's sister, Summer, who came in, kicking two empty boxes, her arms filled with more. "Thanks for the help, Mark." She said and slammed the door behind her. "I guess you know why I'm here."

The sound of my fingers tapping on the keyboard answered her. We never liked each other before and we sure as fuck didn't have any sudden love after the funeral.

Summer went straight to the bedroom and started filling up the boxes with Lanie's things. I could hear the clink of the hangers as she pulled them from the closet, the sound of drawers opening, the shuffle of fabric and the empty slamming broke the stony silence that had fallen on the apartment. Funny, I never noticed until now how quiet it all had become.

Summer didn't say a word to me as she loaded all of Lanie's earthly treasures into her truck and I returned her gesture. After the third trip, she stood at the door, holding the last box, waiting for my attention.

"I'm done here."

"I suppose I will have to trust you." I said, my eyes never leaving the monitor. "I don't have time to make sure nothing of mine got mixed up in there."

"You're a real piece of work, Mark. Don't you feel anything for Lanie?"

"It was her decision. She left, not me."

"Jesus, it's all about you, isn't it? Hey, you know what? Here," she said, throwing the box at my head. "Why don't you check this?!" The box fell short but crashed into the back of my laptop monitor, slamming it shut and fell to the floor and split open like a piñata.

"Hey, watch it! I'm working here!"

Summer smiled and flipped me the bird and slammed the door.

I was left fuming. Lanie's people were maniacs! Inbred circus freaks. Who throws boxes? Like a monkey in the zoo, throwing clumps of shit. Jesus, how did I ever marry into that?

Forget it, man, keep focused. Spreadsheets. We gotta get these books done. We lost valuable time because of Lanie. Focus, man, focus! My fingers dutifully began typing in figures but my eyes kept wandering over to the mess that lay just beyond the table. A jumble of stuff, junk, God only knows what, lying there all over the place, everything, everywhere-

Shit. It was useless. I could never focus surrounded by all that mess. It was up to me, as usual, to clean up Lanie's mess.

I sat down in ground zero and started the clean up. Chapstick, hairbrushes, hair gel. Why the hell would she want this? Matches. Some crap paperback novels. I picked up a thick hardcover There were a dozen colored tabs, sticking out like a gay pride porcupine, bookmarking pages. *How to Keep the Spark.* Oh, man, what is this? I flipped through and saw she had highlighted passages in bright pink. Of course, she would ruin a perfectly good book with pink marker. *"Leave behind pieces of yourself,"* one pink passage read, *"scents your man can find on the trail. Men love the hunt. Don't be afraid to be the hunted".* Oh, Lanie, Lanie. Candles. Pens. Oooh, a notebook. Interesting. Did Lanie keep a journal? I thumbed through a few pages: all blank. Typical Lanie. I tossed it in the box with the rest of the her stuff.

A flash of silver caught my eye. A thumb drive? Where did it come from? A cold wave ripped through me: what if it was one of my old thumb drives from work? Lanie could have found it while cleaning the house and just dumped it in a drawer. Shit, could I have been that careless? Considering how much of a diversion Lanie had been in the past year, it was completely possible. I could get my ass royally chewed out if I had left sensitive account information just lying around.

"Only one way to know for sure, buddy-boy." I said and popped it into the USB port.

There was only one file. A movie file. I right-clicked and opened "Properties".

Created: Tuesday, September 14, 2013, 7:00:45 a.m.

Modified: Tuesday, September 14, 2013, 7:00:55 a.m.

Accessed: Today, December 1, 2013, 1:15:23 p.m.

I clicked on "Summary".

Author: Lanie Matthews

My curiosity got the better of me. I opened the file.

The picture wobbled as she adjusted the camera. She looked into the camera, the screen full of her denim-blue eyes. She sat down and looked at something off-screen. Her eyes widened and she did a double-take, like most people do when they see themselves for the first time on television. *Oh my God, do I really look like that?* She laughed, ran her fingers through her hair, and, then, she froze. She went from laughing Lanie to a cardstock cutout, her corn-silk hair tangled around, strangling her slender fingers.

The movie ended. Ten seconds.

The screen was full of her. Her face, her hair, her smile, the way one side of her mouth would crinkle higher than the other, giving her smile a mischievous bite. Her hair, a pale yellow, so pale it almost looked white in the sunlight, tossled over her forehead, her blue eyes playing peek-a-boo beneath the bangs that she always let grow too long.

I traced the outline of her face on the monitor screen, my fingertips leaving behind ghostly contrails.

Loss, I always believed, belonged on the debit side of Life's accounting grid. Therefore, I figured, I should feel a vacuum, something missing but I did not. Where there should be a hole, there was a jagged rock that rolled around inside me, up and down, side to side, spiking and gouging my guts with each spin.

It *hurt.*

I hurt.

And I hated her for that.

Anger flowed into my belly, coating it like a thick red ichor, wrapping itself all around the jagged ball Lanie had left behind, until only a heaviness remained behind, to remind me that it was even there at all.

I took in a deep breath and exhaled very slowly. *Good boy, Mark. Time to focus on what's important. Hit those spreadsheets.*

I reached to pull out the thumbdrive but as I touched it, a sharp electric shock pricked my finger. "What the hell?"

The screen went black.

"Oh, hell. No!" I picked up the laptop and groaned. "Don't tell me there was a virus on that drive! All my work is on that hard drive! Oh, for chrissakes!"

The screen flicked back to life. Lanie's face once again filled the screen. Suddenly, there was a POP, the sick smell of sulphur and I jumped, nearly dropping the computer.

The movie began again.

Lanie finished tossing her hair back and stared straight into the camera. Her eyes locked on mine.

"Happy Anniversary, baby." She said, smiling that sleepy, lopsided grin. "Remember how you said you wouldn't be home to celebrate with me? Well, I thought I'd slip a little something in your briefcase and surprise you-"

She froze again. Laney looked back him slightly askewed, the tip of her tongue was jutting out, a small dash of pale pink between her red lips.

"I don't have time for this." I yanked the thumb drive and

received a shock three times more powerful than before. "Fuck!" I cursed and shook my throbbing hand, my fingers tingling painfully with electricity.

The screen went black again. There was definitely something wrong with Lanie's thumbdrive. Even beyond the grave, she was ruining everything.

"Shit." I held down the power button for a few seconds until I heard the computer shut down. I gingerly tapped the thumb drive. No shock. I tried to pull it out but it wouldn't budge.

I jumped at the sound of the chimes as the computer powered itself back on.

"What the hell?"

The screen flickered and the logo of Enviroscan Waste Industries popped up. I pecked at a few random keys on the keyboard. Nothing. I gently traced a circle on the mouse touchpad and the cursor swirled around the screen. Everything seem to work okay. I took a deep breath and exhaled slowly. *Okay, then. It was just a glitch. Nothing to get worked up on. Now, let's get back to work. Get focused on those figures, boy! Remember what it is important here.*

I clicked on my spreadsheet folder and it opened for a brief second before there was another POP and that horrible fart smell again. The screen was filled with Laney's sloppy smile and the movie continued. "….with something you can't ignore, baby."

She made a kiss at the camera and laughed nervously and then stood far enough away so her entire body was in frame. She was wearing a sheer, pink baby doll negligee. The frilly top barely skirted past her matching pink glittery thong. She looked off screen to check herself on the monitor and anxiously readjusted her bustline. She smiled, bit her lip and started singing.

Dear God, she started singing. It was the song I always associate with that bobbled headed Betty Boop doll.

And then, dear God, she started dancing.

Lanie ran her hands over her hips, up towards her chest and through her hair, singing, "All I want to be is loved by you! Loved by you! Loved by you!" And then she posed, puckered and-

Oh, please, for the love of God, don't-

"Boop-Boop-Be Do!" and she blew a kiss at the camera.

I covered my face with my hands as she started up another round. This time she pulled a feather boa into the act.

Make it stop…

"I want to be loved by you!" she shimmied, "You and only you…"

Suddenly, a familiar laughter rose over her singing. I peeked through my fingertips. It was me. There I was, in my favorite power suit, suitcases by my feet, laughing at her. "Jesus, Lanie," my screen self said. "What the hell are you doing

Oh God, now I remember.

The conference in Atlanta. It was on our anniversary and she wanted to go so badly. She even asked for it as an anniversary gift. I told her that spouses were not allowed. It was a lie. I just didn't want to miss cruising the Atlanta nightlife with the boys from Fiscal Review.

I had to remind myself to breathe. Shit. How did I forget

that?

On the screen, Lanie jumped at the sound of the door closing and then stood there, just stood there, for what felt like a thousand heartbeats, staring down at the floor. She slowly went to the computer, clicked on the mouse-pad and walked off screen.

She thought she turned it off. She just minimized it!

The camera kept recording the empty room. The couch. A wall of bookcases. Silk flowers and framed art. The only movement came from the fish as they swam back and forth in the aquarium, stage left.

I fast forwarded it. Lanie walked jerkily in the screenshot and then out, oblivious to the camera. *She had forgotten it!* I kept fastforwarding Lanie as she wandered in and out of frame. She had put on her usual house attire, gray sweat-pants and sweatshirt.

Forward, forward, forward.

Lanie came into view, cradling the telephone to her cheek. I pressed PLAY.

"No, no, Mom. Really. It's okay. Okay? I just wanted to call. I just wanted you to know how much-" and she walked off screen, out of range.

Forward, forward, forward.

Lanie's figure popped back on screen. She stood to the side, not moving. As she began moving towards the cam-era, I pressed PLAY.

She sat in front of the computer, blissfully unaware of the camera. Her face was puffy from crying, her hair just pulled up in a messy bun. I felt the hard ball in my stomach roll as she looked into the camera, her dead eyes, flat like a ragdoll's looking into mine.

She looked away, down at the screen. I heard the dull clickety-clack of the keyboard as she began writing.

"Oh God, no." The ball in my stomach, now jagged and sharp, ripped into me as I realized what she was writing.

Dear Mark. I am so sorry. I tried. I really tried but-

I dug my nails into my thighs, the pain pushing back the memory. "No, no, no, no. This isn't real. Not real. It can't be!"

The memory pushed its way through.

I've worn away my fingertips trying to climb up your mountain. I can't climb any higher. You are so far above me, you can't see me anymore. I'm sorry. I tried.

    Love you forever,

    Your Lanie.

She reached for something off screen.

"No…"

She put the barrel, small and gray, under her chin.

"No!" I gripped the thumb drive, ignored the scorching pain and pulled *hard*. I felt it burn ridges into my thumb. There was a sharp CRACK and puff of dark smoke that smelled of shit as it finally came out. I threw it across the room

Her face still filled the screen. Her blank eyes stared back at me with a frozen glare.

Her gaze shifted.

She looked right at me. It wasn't possible, I know, but I could feel her, I could feel the force of her eyes drilling through me.

"Happy anniversary, baby."

And the hot, jagged ball in my gut melted, eating its way through my body as I felt the grief rush through my veins. It hurt. God, it hurt….I hurt….*she* hurt so much.

"Lanie, I'm so sorry." I grabbed the laptop and shook it. "Can you hear me? I said I was sorry! Please! Forgive me!"

Lanie smiled and blew me a kiss. "Here's something you can't ignore, baby."

And then she pulled the trigger.

Again and again and again.

So, do you understand? I still see her. I can't stop seeing her. Everywhere. That sloppy smile. Those denim blue eyes. The horrible splash of red as the back of her head explodes. All the time. On every television screen or computer monitor. I've even started to hear her voice wheedling out to me from speakers, over intercoms and through cellphones.

Especially cellphones.

Can't you hear her?

The End

THE ANSWER
BELL

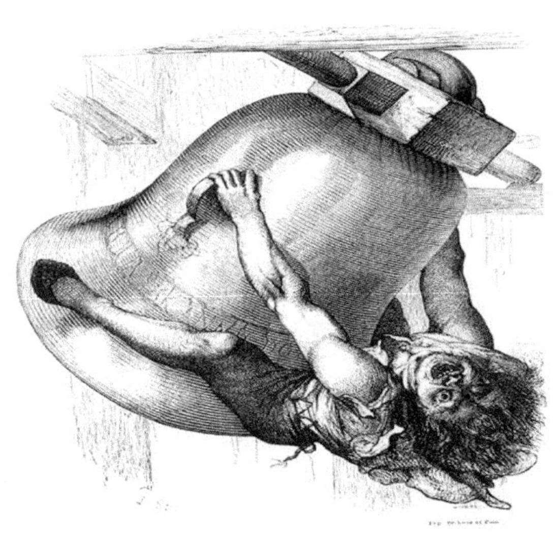

For NWG

October 30, 11:30 p.m.

It was the teeth that caught my eye.

They glistened like a bleached streak against the black charred flesh. The head was frozen in a scream that howled up to the full moon. My eyes moved down to the kneeling body, melted breasts and arms that ended in stumps. The hands were buried in such a way as to seem as if they had melted into the soil.

Agent Wilson touched me on the shoulder, startling me.

"Jesus, Wilson!"

"I figured they'd send you, Ghoul. This shit is right up your alley."

My name is Todd Gould. I am an agent with the Tennessee Bureau of Investigations, Occult Crime Division hence the fun nickname. It's a small team consisting of yours truly. That's what a liberal arts diploma with an emphasis in religious anthropology will get you, folks. Learn from my mistake.

The division was founded during the 80's Satanic day care hullabaloo. So, how are we still being funded in the 21st century? The scuttlebutt is the OCD was kept around just to keep the Religious Right happy. This being Tennessee that could very well be the case. I'm happy to keep my pension.

We were standing in the center of the amphitheater, a half-circle of eight rows of stone seats in the Bicentennial Mall, a tourist site that details the history of Tennessee. The rest of the park sprawls outward with sidewalks lined by endangered willow oak trees, a lawn of luscious grass they keep green even in October ending with the Circle of Three Stars, fifty Doric columns that house a carillon that chimes the Tennessee Waltz every hour.

Interesting factoid I learned during my summer job as a tour guide: there are 95 bells, one bell for each county. A single bell on Capitol Hill just down the road rings at the end of each waltz. It's called the Answer Bell because it symbolizes the Legislature answering the call of the People. Whatever. Frankly, I'd be happier with fewer taxes.

"Humor me, Wilson, and fill in the blanks."

"911 got a call from some Vandy students walking through the park after hitting some bars on Lower Broad. 911 called Metro who got the Park Rangers involved. They called us. I took one look at knew I had to bring you to the party."

"Burnt corpses do not occult make."

"But we have a witness." He jabbed a thumb over his shoulder at a young man shivering in a gray blanket. "The goth punk next to the Ranger. Says the vic was his mother."

"Ouch."

"He's all yours, Ghoul." Wilson said, waving as he walked away. "Welcome to the party."

I bribed the Ranger with the promise of hot coffee for a chance to be alone with the boy. The temperature was dropping and there was an odd, electric prickling in the air. I looked at my wristwatch; it had stopped dead at 11:15. "Hey! Ranger! What time do you have?" He pulled out an old fashioned pocket watch. Nice. I've always wanted one. He shrugged. "I must've forgotten to wind it."

The boy was perhaps fourteen. He had the blanket pulled up over his shoulders and curled around him so tightly he looked like a burrito. Tufts of raven hair popped out of the top as he shook and sobbed. Or at least I thought he was sobbing. As I got closer, I could hear he was laughing.

"Excuse me." I flashed my badge. "I'm Agent Gould, TBI. Can I ask you a few questions?"

"Fire away!" he said and laughed a high pitch giggle.

"How did you know the victim?"

The boy sat up straight, the blanket falling around him. His eyes were wide and manic. Glassy. I made a mental note to have them run a tox screen.

"She was the One who would come clothed in the Sun!" he screamed.

Hoooo boy. I've seen cult shit like this before. Poor kid. He slumped down as I sat down next to him and pulled the blanket back over his shoulder. A book tumbled out of his lap. He grabbed for it, but I got to the book first.

Der Vermis Mysteriis.

What the hell? I pulled out my flashlight and looked closer at the binding. Leather. No, not leather. Skin. Probably human. Darkened by age but I could see the telltale sign of a nipple in the crease. He did not find this at Hot Topic.

"Where did you get this?"

The boy slumped further into the blanket, like a gray womb. "It doesn't matter. Soon nothing will matter."

There was a satin bookmark. I turned to the page and saw a hermetic design and instructions for a ritual. *The Axis of Meru.*

"Is this what you did? This ritual? Is this what fried your

mother?"

He sat up straight. "She is the One who is clothed in Sun!"

"Yeah, yeah. At ease, soldier boy." I took the book and walked the outline of the amphitheater. Walking helps me put the puzzles together and find the connections. Damn! I know I have seen this design somewhere. My Latin was rusty but it's better than my German. There were a few words I could make out in the invocation: stars, beyond, unnamed, opening and sacrifice. Nice. You simply can't go wrong with a juicy sacrifice.

It was a typical summoning ritual, open the door and let the nasties from Outside of Time and Space into our world. Yadda Yadda. Typical Lovecraft shit.

But the design looked disturbingly familiar. It bugged me, tagged at something in my brain.

The Park Ranger came back with a cup of coffee. "What's the story? Did she grab a hot electrical line or what? We've got a running pool back at the office."

I showed him the diagram. "Does this ring a bell?"

His head cocked to the side and he looked like a bewildered basset hound. And then a light came on. "Hold on a minute!" He ran back to the souvenir shop. He came back with a map of the Bicentennial Mall. He placed it alongside the diagram. "I knew it. They are the same, aren't they?"

My forehead broke out in a cold sweat. I ran up the eight steps of the amphitheater and looked down the center of the park. I look, trembling, back to the book. "Oh, Mother of God…what have you done?"

"She is the One who will come clothed in the Sun!" the

boy screamed from behind me. I nearly dropped the book from shock. "The Bride's Veil will be ripped at the time of the Thinnest. The Door has been opened and the Bride prepared!"

The Ranger slapped the boy. He crumpled down to the ground, laughing and weeping.

The story was unfolding in my mind. Sacred Geometry. There was a conspiracy theory that in many major cities, the layouts were based on alchemical symbols. Some kind of Illuminati/Masonic shit. I had read about it but…it was insane. Wasn't it?

Yet, there it was. Right in front of me. The Bicentennial Mall in the shape of the Axis of Meru, a key to the Door.

Coincidence? Conspiracy? This boy, his mother and, from the discarded backpacks, a group of believers had performed the ritual. But to summon what? And why now? My mind force fed me the answer: the time of the thinnest. Halloween. The time when the veil between our world and the next is at its-

I turned to the Ranger. "Does anyone have a watch that works?"

"Mine's run down but the carillon rings every hour. Should be hitting midnight soon."

No, no, no, no. This can't be real. It's impossible! My mind screamed. I turned to look at the boy, my only confidante. He giggled miserably and started crying as the bells started chiming.

The tones started a rumbling that cracked through the sky. There was a tear in the nighttime veil, darkening the stars, and swallowing any other night sound. The wind took on a malevolent force and whipped through the park, tossing benches and trash cans.

I crouched down by a stone step. Dark shapes, flapping things, flew through the rift and perched in the trees. The Ranger stood dumbfounded; he never noticed the boy grabbing for his gun. The boy shot once, under his chin straight through his skull. It was probably the smartest thing he had ever done.

The crack of the shot startled the birdthings into flight and they circled around the amphitheater, a dozen of them, a hundred, too many to count, until they created a black funnel cloud that hung high above the Ranger. The cloud twisted and swirled as if it were in the throes of childbirth. A screaming started high in the sky and sharpened as it came down the funnel. The sound roared out and slammed into the Ranger's chest, tearing away his beige uniform, ripping a hole straight through his body. The Ranger fell backwards, his head cracking on the stone step beside me. Finished, the funnel melted away into a thousand flapping shapes that broke off and perched back into the trees.

The Carillion bells stopped and a thick silence filled the park. I looked skyway and saw a few twinkling stars that remained defiant alongside the yellow moon. "Is that it?" I stood and screamed out to the rip in dark sky. I felt my blood beat in my ears. "Is that all you can do?"

A low, deep, bass note that came from behind me. It was what we all want when we pray, I suppose.

The Answer Bell responded.

And the last of the lights flickered and died.

The End

STONE BABY

A Southern Gothic Triptych

For Dana

Clayton

The old black woman threw small rocks at Clayton Lankford as he clipped the hedge at Miss Dellie Dodd's house. The guys back at the shop had warned him about her. "Watch out for that old bitch, the Goose," they said. "Something happened way back between her and Mr. Mac and she'll go out of her way to make trouble."

Clayton tried to ignore the stinging as the tiny rocks bit into his bare back but when one came buzzing by his ear nearly hitting him in the eye, that took it too far. "Okay, that's enough!" He tossed his clippers and turned to face her. "Stop throwing rocks at me!"

"I will when you put a shirt on. Have some respect for yo'self. Or at least some common decency for those of us havin' to look at your skinny white ribs."

The Goose came over to the chain link fence that separated the properties and leaned against it. Her wrinkled, brown skin hung off her bones like leathery drapes. Clayton instantly felt shame for yelling at her. He could tell she was sick. The same kind of sick that took his own granny two years ago.

"I ain't kiddin' about that shirt, Boy. Put something on. You're going to give Dellie fits. She's been watchin', you know. She's always at those winders, watching."

"Yes, ma'am." He pulled his yellow 'McAdoo Can-Do Lawn Services' t-shirt out of his back pocket where he'd stuffed it and put it on. In spite of the heat, Clayton couldn't go against a lifetime of his Momma's training to always respect your elders. He picked up the clippers and started back on the hedges, working even harder to get finished as quickly as possible.

"Shit. I don't know why y'all even worry about them hedges. Let 'em grow. Taller the better, I say. Keeps me from having to look at that eyesore of a house." The Goose spit out a dark stream of tobacco juice. "It's a damn shame. I knew her momma, Miss Marcia. That woman, Lord have mercy, what a sorry hand of cards she was dealt." She started counting them out on knobby, arthritic fingers. "First, a no count husband that took off, not that most men are of any count no ways anyhow." She counted off a second finger, shaking her head, "And to be left with that girl, Dellie, for a daughter. I said to my man, Gerald, 'a slut, that one is.' When her momma took in lodgers, that girl took her a little something-something too. Her momma knew. Don't believe for a second she didn't. Suspect that's what killed her. Don't look at me that way, boy. My man, Gerald, said it too. No woman that lets herself get used that way is right."

"I wouldn't know anything about that, ma'am. Mr. Mac just sent me to do the hedges."

" Hershel McAddo." The woman's face darkened as she spit out the name. "Lissen up to me, boy. You be careful of what you do for that man. My Gerald, he did jobs for him, too. I don't know what, my man never had the stomach to tell me, but whatever it was, it killed him." The Goose grunted and kicked at the fence. "Hershel didn't pull the trigger but he sure as hell gave Gerald the bullets to shoot hisself."

Clayton stopped in mid-clip. "What?"

"Nothing. I ain't said nothing you need to be worried about." Goose waved him away. "Whatcha'll ought to be worrying about is that big damn tree out front. It ain't nothing but a shell. It's dead, rotten as that house but, does anyone do anything? Noooooosir, they just keep trimming the hedges. Let the hedges grow high! Then maybe she won't be at them winders watching people. I see her do it. She's been watching you. You know that, right? Standing right there at those winders, watching the world through her peeping eyes. It's agin the law, ain't it? To watch on neighbors? And she steals my roses, right off the bushes. Sneaks out like some damn catburgler and clips off roses through the fence. I seen her do it. Now that's gots to be agin the law!"

"I wouldn't know. Sorry." Clayton shook his head and let the whole who-shot-Gerald question fade away. It was sad how old people went crazy. He quickly finished the last hedge and started bagging up the clippings. He felt that weird tingling at his shoulder and turned towards the house. He caught a glimpse of a hand pulling away.

"Well, I watch her, too. It's just as well. I see her, up in the winder there on the top floor. She walks back and forth, swaying like she's dancing, holding something close. I even heard her singing once, a few weeks back when she put the windows down to catch a summer breeze. She was cooing out lullabyes. Lullabyes!" The Goose cawed out a laugh. She spit out another brown stream and shook her head. "Can you believe anything more crazy?"

Clayton bent over to stuff the last of the trimmings into a burlap sack. He wiped his brow and looked at the sky. The sun was around 4 o'clock but there were dark clouds on the horizon and the breeze had a steel edge that promised a nasty storm was brewing.

The Goose kept on talking while Clayton pulled out his phone and texted Mr. Mac that he was ready for pickup. He nodded and smiled at what he hoped were appropriate moments. She never lost a beat so either they were, or she didn't give a damn either way.

Ten minutes later, Mr. Mac drove up in his truck. The Goose spit and pulled herself away from the fence. "You tell Hershel what I told you about that tree. It's gonna crash into that dead old house and when it does, don't say I didn't say it wouldn't." She raised up her hands in absolution. "And that's all I gots to say!"

A shiver ran down Clayton's neck. *There it was again!* That feeling he was being watched. He refused to look over at the house. He picked up the bag and tossed it over his shoulder. He kept his back straight as he walked to the truck.

He heard the high squeal of a storm door opening.

The guys at the shop said that Miss Dellie Dodd was circus freak ugly. Like a squishy toad, Marcus said, with a pig nose, tits that swung down to her crotch and crusty toenails on her feet.

No, no, no. Not gonna look. No.

The door slammed and he stopped dead. He thought he heard a sound, a clicking sound. A kerchunky sound like a shotgun being readied to fire a load into his backside.

HONK HONK! Clayton jumped and involuntarily cut one loose at the sound of the truck's horn. He reached back and wiped his ass to make sure he hadn't shit himself.

"Hey there, boy!" Mr. Mac called out from the cab. "You finished?"

He felt dry and breathed deeply for the first time all day. "Yessir!" He picked up the burlap sack, ran, and tossed it into the bed of the truck.

"Careful! See those grocery bags?"

"Yessir?"

"Help me carry them inside to Miss Dodd."

Clayton's heart dropped. "Yessir."

McAdoo

Hershel McAdoo turned off the ignition and heaved his body out of the cab. He prayed as his feet hit the road, *I know I'm all the girl has left in the world but, Lord, this is getting to be too much of a burden.*

"Clayton! Careful! There's eggs in those bags!"

"Yessir."

McAdoo shook his head. Clayton was skinny and none too damn sharp, but the boy wanted to please and, as far as McAdoo cared, that was enough. He remembered how it was, to be forced out into the world with nothing. Right out of high school, McAdoo learned the ins and outs of groundskeeping and moved up to construction. When his old boss retired, McAdoo bought him out and learned the convoluted game of government grants. It was a good gig and some years he made more than his cousin with the Ph.D. That always made McAdoo smile. No, he couldn't recite Shakespeare but he could build a house. Which one would keep a man dry during a thunderstorm? Education, eh.... shit on it.

McAdoo made his way to the sidewalk. His hip was giving him hell again, making him walk like a damn gimp, like someone had sawn off one leg shorter than the other. A storm was coming. Getting old was one thing but becoming a goddamn weather barometer was never in the brochure.

He did a sideways glare over towards that old bitch, Lacey Dubois. She was sitting on her porch, shaking her head and cursing him under his breath. He couldn't hear it, but he knew she was doing it all the same. Her man, Gerald, did odd jobs for him, back in the day. Little things he couldn't get a white man to do. And one time, a job a Christian man didn't want to get his hands dirty doing. He wasn't proud of it, no, but sometimes a sick dog had to be put down and Dwayne Dodd was such a dog, no argument. If Dwayne figured out that the baby in Marcia's belly wasn't his, McAdoo didn't want to think what would've happened to the woman he loved.

It was easy. Scrawny little shitstick like Dwayne went down without a throwing a punch. Gerald snapped his neck like a Christmas goose, hid the body in his root cellar.

Gerald didn't like stashing the body at his house, but McAdoo kept him under his thumb. *It's only for a few days so keep quiet or I'll call the police on you. Who are they going to believe? A local businessman or a felon with a dead white man in his root cellar?*

Gerald kept his mouth closed with a bottle.

Four days later, McAdoo Landscaping put in the boxwood hedge on the Dodd's property that became the envy of the neighborhood.

It's amazing what you can hide in plain sight.

The hedge was still there. McAdoo noted that Clayton did a good job trimming it up. You could barely notice the slight dip in the ground towards the middle where the ground had settled. No matter what McAdoo did to fill that gap, it wouldn't go away. He figured that was all the otherworldly justice a dumb shit like Dwayne Dodd could muster up.

Clayton shifted the bags. "Do you want me to take these up to the porch, sir?"

"No. I've got business with Miss Dodd today. Complaints about the oak tree again. Metro wants me to cut it down."

"I heard what happened last time Metro came out to just trim two of her trees. She came out with an axe, ran off the Metro guys and cut them down herself."

The jagged stumps of the two tulip poplars were still there, testament to what happened when Miss Dellie Dodd didn't get her way. "You weren't talking to that old bitch next door were you?"

"No, sir." Clayton shuffled his feet, the heavy plastic bags cutting into his hands. "The guys at the shop told me."

"Let's get on with it. The sooner we get done before the storm hits."

McAdoo walked up to the door, noticing the peeling yellow paint on the porch posts and the stucco flower pots filled with dead plants. The weather faded "Rooms to Let" sign still hung by the door. He wrinkled his nose at the horrible smell of cat piss. McAdoo felt a sick wave of shame rise from his belly.

He knocked on the door. "Dellie girl? Are you home?"

No answer. He knocked again, waited and then pulled out the keys from when he did odd jobs for Marcia's boarding house. He listened to the click of the deadbolt.

"Dellie?" He opened the door slowly. Normally, he just left the bags outside. "It's Mr. McAdoo. I brought you some groceries. I need to talk to you about something."

The only answer was the thunder of padded paws running across the floor. Within seconds, dozens and dozens of cats of all colors and sizes rushed the front door.

"AHHH! Son of a bitch!!" the old man screamed as the door was yanked by a tide of cats. He fell to the porch and blocked the door as dozens of cats, many of them wearing lacy baby dresses, and one trailing a frilly bonnet tied to its neck, rolled over him. "Jesus!" he screamed and covered his head against the clawing and hissing felines.

"Mr. Mac!" Clayton dropped the bags and went to the old man's aid. The cats screeched and squirted hot streams of piss as he kicked them out of the way. Clayton tried to help the old man to his feet, but the man's girth was too much for the boy.

"GET AWAY! GET AWAY!" A tornado of white hair and polka dots rushed up to the door, screaming and spitting. "My cats! You bastards let loose my cats!"

Clayton fell back on his ass and his eyes bugged out at the monster in the doorway. Standing over him was a banshee in a purple polka dot housedress. She was fat and squat like a toad. Her face was white and doughy and everything about her looked swollen and ready to pop. The only thing hard about her was her eyes. Twin black pieces of flint pushed in over flabby cheeks glared down at him.

"What are you looking at, pig?!" The monster took a step towards Clayton. Frazzled white hair moved in the air like seaweed in a tidepool. The movement made him dizzy and queasy. He could feel the sick coming up his throat.

"Settle down, Dellie, leave the boy alone." McAdoo got up on his feet and pulled the woman back. "Clayton, get the groceries. Go on, boy. I got this."

Clayton scrambled crablike towards the bags. He gathered

up the spilled cans and jars stuffing them back in the bags, all the while keeping an eye on the banshee at the door.

"I'm sorry about the cats, Dellie, but they'll be back. A storm is coming. You know how cats are."

"Humph." She grunted and pulled at her stomach. "What do you want?"

He pulled out the envelope. "Metro wants me to cut down your oak tree, Dellie."

"What? My tree?" She leaned up against the doorjamb, her face growing paler. "Nonono...they can't take my tree. I won't let them."

"Dellie, listen to me, I know you love your tree but, sweetie, it's a dead husk of a thing. It's a danger to you and your neighbors."

"My great granddaddy planted that tree! It's historic! You can't take it away from me!" She bent over and clutched at her gut. "It's mine." She spit the word through clenched teeth. "MINE!"

McAdoo's throat tightened at the sight of her. She was never a pretty girl but the woman who stood in front of him was hideous. Her skin was waxy and her eyes sunken and glassy. Hershel McAdoo might not have had much schooling but it didn't take a degree to see that there was something very, very wrong with Dellie Dodd.

He bit his lip as he asked, "Dellie girl, are you all right?"

"Uuuugh. Go away...just go away."

 McAddo touched her on the shoulder. "Let me help you, sweetheart."

Dellie reared back like a cat, slapped at his hand, and hissed. "Don't. Touch. Me. Just… go away!" She grappled with the doorknob, using one hand, the other one cradling her stomach. She opened the door and stepped inside. "GO AWAY!! We don't need you!" she shouted, slamming the door shut.

McAdoo knocked. "Dellie? Dellie! Answer me."

The sound of something heavy enough to shake the frame crashing into the door answered him.

McAdoo stood there stunned, blinking.

"Mr. Mac?"

McAdoo turned to see Clayton holding up the bags of groceries.

"Just leave them by the door."

"Hope she comes to get them soon. The wind is picking up." Clayton propped the bags up. "Sir, I promised Mom I'd be home by five and it's nearing 4:30."

"Fine. Fine." McAdoo, looked back at the house. He wasn't sure what he was looking for. A sign, maybe? Something…just something.

The light went off in the front room.

So be it, Lord.

"Let's get you home. Nothing more to be done here."

As they walked to the truck, Clayton said, "Mr. Mac, she doesn't still rent out rooms, does she?"

McAddo shook his head.

"Then what did she mean by 'we'? She wasn't talking about the cats, do you think?"

"Maybe." Out of the corner of his eye, he saw Lacey Dubois jut her jaw out and spit as a fat raindrop fell on his face and trailed down his cheek.

Dellie

Dellie Dodd held her breath and counted to ten as the footsteps died away. She released her breath and opened the door a crack to peek outside.

They were gone. Good.

To her left, there were three white plastic bags, flapping in the wind. She looked, right to left, and seeing no one, slipped out as quickly as her girth would allow, snatched up the groceries and brought them inside.

"It's okay, Baby, it's okay now." She leaned against the door to catch her breath. She rubbed the small lump in her belly, feeling it roll beneath her hand. "Let's go see what Uncle Hershel brought us today."

Dellie swept the broken pieces of the plate she had thrown with her foot, making a mental note to clean it up later. Her mental housekeeping notes were starting to pile up. Dishes to wash, floors to sweep, trash to take out, so many goddamn things to dust. No matter how hard Dellie tried to keep the place clean, the bones of the house shown through. Mother would not be pleased with the state of the house. Oh, no. The cracks in the leather on Father's chair was a roadmap that connected all the cigarette burns. Mother's antique dollhouses sat unloved, with a blanket of dust and cat hair covering them like snow. The cats. Oh, Mother would not have loved the cats. Between the hair and the smell, Mother would not have been pleased at all.

But that bitch was rarely pleased, was she? All those nights when the house was empty of guests and she was full of booze, Mother would come into her bedroom and slap Dellie with a belt. "It's all your fault, Dellie-girl. If you hadn't taken root in my gut, things would've been different. Things would've been so much different!"

She rubbed her belly and smiled.

Her baby would never have to hide under thick blankets so the buckle wouldn't hurt so much. Her baby would never have to push the chest of drawers in front of the door to stay safe. No one would ever laugh, poke or smack her baby. Dellie Dodd was a good mother; she protected her baby.

She made her way to the kitchen and emptied the bag. Canned vegetables, canned soup, a gallon of milk, a dozen eggs, three loaves of bread, a bag of potatoes and three pounds of pre-packaged chicken breasts. Dellie slowly put everything away into their proper places. With each step, her swollen feet ached. She made a mental note to put some Epsom salt in her bath. "That will be nice, won't it, Baby? I'll dribble water on your head and sing the raindrops song. Won't that be fun?"

Dellie felt a shifting in her belly. The shifting turned into a sharp stabbing. Grunting, she took a deep breath and released it, dulling the edge of the pain. "Please, Baby, you're hurting your momma. Please, stop. I know what. Let's go visit your Daddy, okay? Would you like that? And then I'll make us a warm salt bath. Okay?"

The lessening of the cramp in her gut was a message of

agreement for Dellie. She stopped at the staircase and looked up the flight of steps. Ten steps and a landing and then ten more to the second floor. To the right was the master bedroom that used to be Momma's but now it was Dellie's. To the left, were two unused rooms, another bathroom, the nursery and Jeffrey's room.

She started up the stairs, one painful step at a time.

The carpet was matted with hairballs and crusty bits of food the cats had dragged to the landing. She kicked aside a shredded dress a cat torn off in its escape. Dellie couldn't remember when she started dressing the cats. Sometimes for Dellie Dodd, things like that just happened. It was as if there were big, black divots in her head where she couldn't remember exactly what had happened but, strangely, there was always a huge mess to clean up afterwards.

Dressing the cats was the least of those problems.

Ten more steps, a landing and then a few quick feet to Jeffrey's door.

Dust motes danced in the light that streamed through the window. When she was a girl, she would pretend they were fairies who would grant her wishes. She whispered into the swirling cloud, "Make me a princess! Give me long, blonde hair and a diamond crown and pretty, blue eyes." Every day, she would squint her eyes tight and pray so hard, only to open them to the same kinky brown hair and hazel eyes.

A weatherman pointed to a map on the television in the corner. Dellie kept it on as company for Jeffrey. On the dresser were rows of roses in mason jars. The smell had faded years ago but Dellie kept bringing them anyway. He always liked roses. She would bring them on his breakfast tray, back in the day. She tried to keep his room like time was frozen here, as if someone had taped down the pause button on the remote control.

Dellie stood by the bed and looked down at the stick thin figure under the flowery sheet. She tucked the covers under the mattress, tight as a soldier's bunk. The lump in the bed grew smaller each year but, sometimes, Dellie thought she saw it move, ever so slightly.

Tufts of blonde hair that stubbornly clung to the top of his head peeked out from beneath. Dellie remembered how beautiful he looked, back in the day. His curly blonde hair, icy blue eyes and straight white teeth, like an angel poured into denim jeans and cotton t-shirt. He wasn't like the other lodgers who patted her on the ass when they were done and moved on. Jeffrey was special. Her prince. He was the one, she was sure of it. With every condom she pricked with a pin, she was even surer of it. He just needed persuasion to see what she already knew.

Her mind flashed back to that day, so many years ago, that bright morning when she told Jeffrey. They were going to have a family…and then he pulled out his wallet, gave her $200 dollars and told her to "Fix it."

"What?"

"Fix it. Are you stupid? Get an abortion."

"But…Jeffrey…you and me."

"Jesus, seriously? You think I'm going to throw away my future for a stupid fat whore like you? Fix it!"

Fix it. Fix it. FIX IT. The words rumbled through her head, rammed down her throat and seized her heart. FIX IT, he said and turned his back to her. He turned his back to her. That was worse than any punch and then he pulled out his suitcase and started packing. The memory turns wavy after that. He never saw the scissors; she was sure of that. The long, silver, sewing scissors that Momma never allowed Dellie to use but she did have them, yes, oh, hell yes, she had them in her hand, in her fist, right this moment. How? Dellie didn't remember. They appeared magically. Maybe the fairies put them there. Yes. The fairies. It was magic. It was ordained. She slammed the scissors into his back, like a silver crow's beak, over and over, until he fell onto the bed. She leaned over him. The blood bubbled out of his mouth, frothy, red and white, like espresso foam, not like what she imagined at all.

There was a scream, from behind her. It was Mother. She stood there, at the door and screamed. What did she say? Words? Or just a guttural scream of shock? Dellie couldn't recall. Mother fell, that much Dellie knows for sure. Mother saw what she had done, walked down the hallway a bit, fell and never got back up. A stroke took Momma, they said at the hospital.

Then, Dellie was alone to make a house for Baby and herself. She set up the nursery, ordered all the right things she read about in the magazines and waited.

Then it happened. One morning, so many, many years ago, she woke up, her bed soaking wet and the pain and, oh God, the blood. She stayed in bed that entire day, rolling in agony until she prayed to God for the pain to go away. She was sorry, Lord, so sorry for everything. Please God, please make the baby be still, just be still. She passed out but when she woke up, the pain was gone. And her baby, the Baby, was still there. The Baby that stayed. The only one that never left.

"But it will always be just you and me, right?"

Dellie ground her teeth against the pain as another bout

of stabbing ripped through her gut. "Oh, God!" She fell to her knees as a scream escaped through her lips. It was like sharp claws digging out from inside her. The pain ratcheted up a notch and Dellie fell over onto her side and pulled up her knees, holding Baby close, rocking back and forth until the spasm faded away. "It's just you and me…. ohGOD!"

There was a rolling in her gut, as if Baby had turned over, and then only silence.

"Baby?" Dellie Dodd got up to her knees and stayed there, on all fours, panting. "Don't you play games now. You answer your mother."

A lightning strike of pain answered her.

She hugged her belly and moaned. From outside, Dellie heard a sharp crack and a cold black calm flooded over her. She did hear it, didn't she? It wasn't just inside her head? Thunder outside rumbled, shaking the windows. No, the crack was there. It was inside, outside, everywhere. She pulled herself up to her feet. She sobbed as she gripped her swollen belly. "Fine. Just fine. You want out? Is that what you want? So be it."

She stumbled down the stairs, huffing and growling against the pain. Another spasm hit as she reached the bottom and she crumbled, falling hands and knees into the pile of broken ceramic shards. She cried in frustration as she crawled over to her father's cigarette scorched leather chair. Her breath was ragged and sweat rolled into her eyes as she pulled herself up to her feet.

A long bassoon of thunder rolled outside. Dellie turned towards the sound just lightning outlined the shape of her great-granddaddy's tree.

"What?"

Dellie barely had time to speak as the tree crashed through the parlor window, raining shards of glass inside. She laid there for a few minutes, feeling a hot wetness pool around her. Her hands went instinctively to her belly where her fingers traced a five-inch blade of glass jutting out.

"Why did I think you'd be different?"

Her breath heaved and her head swirled in black and reds as she fought to stay conscious. The red behind her eyes solidified and exploded in anger as she grabbed the glass and pulled it across her belly. A torrent of blood and water flooded out, nearly washing away the glass. "You want out?" She pulled the shard downwards until it hit a stony resistance. "Then....GET OUT!"

She rolled over and a river of ropey innards spilled out like a loose ball of yarn. In the middle of it all was a glossy eight-inch baby doll, carved out of marble and curled up as if still peacefully sleeping inside her womb.

"Baby?" All the pain was forgotten. The smell of shit and copper burned her nose as Dellie pushed aside her bloody entrails and pulled the stone baby into her arms. "Oh, Baby. My baby. Look at you." Tears trailed down her face as she traced the perfectly sculptured face with her fingertip. "You are so beautiful...just so perfect...look at your little nose. Your fingers. You are so perfect. You're cold. Don't cry. I'll warm you. Just hush now, Baby.... hush.... sleep now. Just...sleep." She pulled her knees up and cradled the stone baby to her breast. She kissed its forehead and hummed a soft lullaby, her voice weak and fading away in the wind and rain.

The End

THE FIVE STAGES
OF SLEEP

For Leeman & Friends

Hello, friend.

Don't scream.

Please. Don't scream. Or run away. Not that you could; the doors are all locked and only the night nurses are on call. Frankly, you don't want to bother them. It's been my experience, and I have had many, many encounters with such folk, that people who work night shifts are generally the most disagreeable sort. It's the circadian rhythm, you see. Not enough sunlight; it messes with their sense of propriety and, honestly, no one gets paid well enough to put up with shrieks and wet bedsheets at 2 a.m. so calm down.

I need to explain to you what happened and why it happened. It's my way of an apology. I don't have long before the pills you tried to hide under your tongue from the nurse take effect, so pay attention.

There are five stages of sleep. Did you know that?

I heard this one day either on the radio or the television. I couldn't see from where I was lying. You were home from school, sick with chicken pox or mono, one or the other; time isn't easy to measure there under your bed. Hours, days, months, generations can go by. It's all the same to me. Still, I loved those times most of all. The sick days. When you were bedridden, feverish, moored to your bed, the mattress sagging just a little in the middle. I would caress your bottom, or thump it, as the mood struck. Did you feel me? No? That hurts but it doesn't matter. They were our times and I treasure those memories. I enjoyed reading comics books that would slide behind the headboard. And, later, the other magazines you would hide from Mother as your tastes grew more lascivious.

You were such a naughty, naughty boy.

Yet none of those lurid photographs peaked my sense of wonder in me as did those words: There are five stages of sleep. Five? Fascinating.

Normally, I resign myself to the shadows underneath the bedside but being a creature of curiosity with plenty of leisure time at my command, I decided to test this idea. And, luckily, I had a handy, if not knowingly willing, test subject.

You.

And I am terribly sorry. Mea Culpa

It was because of what I learned while watching you go through those stages of sleep that I did what I did and then you did what you did and, well, you know how that ended. I hope you'll forgive me once I explain the situation fully. Ready? Curl up with your pillow and listen.

Stage one: Alpha. That sounds so aloof and academic, doesn't it? Like something carved in Greek letters on a cold, granite mausoleum wall. On the contrary, it's the most pleasant stage of all. That in-between stage where the stress of the day slowly bleeds away and your muscles relax and succumb to the inevitable. It's my favorite stage, to be honest. Our special time where I'd crawl next to you and watch the years melt from your face as the lines faded away and the child whose hair I pulled while he slept reemerged from behind that adult mask.

Interesting fact: during this stage, you are at your most vulnerable, most suggestible. It's like a door and I cross the threshold freely and I am welcomed. During this soft, drowsy time, your brain conjures up fanciful visions of places and hears things, like bells or voices, telling you dark, blood red stories of things that were, things to come and crooked, broken things that should never ever be. Sometimes, the muscles will jerk as if you are saving yourself from a dangerous, imaginary fall.

Here's an insider's tip: it's not imaginary.

Stages two to four are transitional. You go from one to the other, step by step, like a ladder descending into a pit. Your body temperature lowers and your breathing gets slower and slower until it is like you are mimicking death, slipping away, further and further from me. I do my best to follow you through this maze. I want to keep you safe. Remember that. I only wanted you to be safe.

Stage five is the cruelest stage. Your brain is active, dreams flying left and right, yet your body is paralyzed, unable to move, to react, to run away. Do you remember those dreams where the monsters are rushing at you, coming from all four walls and slithering up from the Swiss cheese holes in the floor? Your heart beats faster but you can't run away. Even your voice fails you as try to scream but only small whimpers escape from your lips. Don't deny that; I've heard you. It's so unfair. Don't you think? I do. It broke my heart to see you suffer, my friend. I couldn't stand the injustice any longer.

That's why I unlocked you. I pulled a few synapses here, blew a magic word into your ear and gave you the gift to react, to run, to get the .45 magnum gun you keep in the dresser drawer by your bed when you travel and fight back.

Who knew hotel walls were that thin? That bullets could travel that far?

So, you see, in my defense, despite the unpleasantness for the family in the room next door, the police, the trial, sentenced to this institution, what I did, I did out of love for you, really.

Anyway, that's all I wanted to say. I can tell by the way your eyes are struggling to focus on me, the medicine is taking effect. I'm glad we got to talk, at least for a few minutes. I hope I helped. I hope you remember in the morning.

And don't worry about the nightmares. I hear the pills stop you from dreaming.

Mostly.

And don't be lonely. I'll be under there, in the shadows.

Always.

The End

114

Nikki Nelson-Hicks has been described as the "Undisputed Queen of the Warped and the Weird" and the "unholy child of H.P. Lovecraft and Flannery O'Connor."

She finds both terribly amusing.

All her books can be found on Amazon in paperback and Kindle.

nikkinelsonhicks@gmail.com